Meerkat Madness

IAN WHYBROW

Illustrated by Sam Hearn

HarperCollins *Children's Books*

Also available by Ian Whybrow

Little Wolf's Book of Badness

For Judith Bows, Library Supremo, and all the children of ICS, Zurich and especially for Abbie, Lara and Caroline, who asked me to do an adventure story for them; for Nilou who likes yellow, Esther who likes dark blue and Maria and Malti who prefer purple.

Beginning

Down...

Deeper than that...

A very long way down
under the burning sand
of the Kalahari desert...

at the end of a branch-line
in a meerkat-burrow

that led off the main tunnel

there was

a dark

(private)
chamber.

In the chamber, three meerkat kits were squeezed up close on their uncle's lap, because this was in fact a nursery.

Once Uncle Fearless had been a king; now he was their babysitter. That is the meerkat way when things go badly.

One of Uncle's eyes was missing and his fur was a bit patchy and ragged in places. His left arm had an unusual bend in it. "War wounds, what-what!" he would often explain. He had not lost his royal pride.

This secret nursery was completely dark. Once or twice Uncle had shown the kits how to dig away the thick sand that served as their main door, but there was no light in the tunnels outside. So the kits had not yet seen what their uncle looked like.

He had just come down from the Upworld with supper. He hadn't had much time to forage, for a fierce sandstorm was raging outside the safe fortress of the burrow. Still, he had brought them each some worms. And for a treat, there was a plump Flap-Neck Chameleon to share. Delicious!

"Make us big and strong!" piped Little Dream. He was growing fast but he was by far the smallest of the kits. That meant he was always last in line.

He was born a moment or two before his brother and sister, Skeema and Mimi, but they had always treated him like the baby. He often seemed slow, he talked in a strange way, and, to tell the truth, they thought he was a bit dim.

Uncle wanted the kits to settle down and go to sleep. "For *tomorrow*," he promised them, "you must all be ready to leave the nursery and join the rest of the tribe!"

How they squeaked and squealed and squirmed when they heard that! They weren't at all sure that they wanted to leave the safe and cosy darkness. It wasn't easy for Uncle to calm them down, and he had to put on his warning voice before they settled.

"Don't worry," he said. "It'll be fun." He told them that there were some older, more important kits in the burrow; some princes and a princess. Now that Skeema, Mimi and Little Dream were old enough, he was ready to lead them personally along the tunnels to the Upworld and introduce them. And then, if they were very good, they would meet the King and Queen.

"You'll be able to *see* them," said Uncle. "It's like smelling with your eyes. The sun will show you how. It's lovely."

"And will we see you?" asked Skeema.

"Oh, yes. As a matter of fact I look wonderfully handsome in sunlight," he answered. The kits weren't sure what that meant. Still, for the moment they were happy just to know that he was there to defend them and that he had a sharp and special smell that they were very fond of. They could not remember their mother, Princess Fragrant. She had been taken by a wild dog when they were just three days old. They could *just* remember Flower who had nursed them and fed them milk in the very early times. But it was

15

Uncle whom they loved. Even if he did puff himself up, he meant the world to them.

"Tell Mimi a story," said Mimi, cuddling up. "Me! Me!"

"Not just Mimi. Tell all of us!" begged Skeema.

"Blah-blahs," said Little Dream.

"Yes," said Skeema, "Tell us about the Blah-blahs."

Chapter 1

There was nothing Uncle liked better than to talk about his Glory Days.

He cleared his throat importantly. "Harrumph! This story is called 'The Adventures of Bold King Fearless Among the Blah-blah Tribes'," he announced.

As usual, the kits asked, "Why are they called Blah-blahs, Uncle?"

And as usual he laughed and said, "Because of the funny calls they make to each other, of course! *Blah-blah-blah-blah-blah!*"

The kits laughed and squirmed happily. Little Dream picked a fat flea off his sister and nibbled it thoughtfully while he listened.

"Now, once upon a suntime," said Uncle, "I left the safety of Far Burrow where I lived, at the far edge of the Land of the Sharpeyes, and set off to explore the Upworld. I wanted to travel and to learn all I could about my kingdom. At first the rest of the tribe insisted that I took bodyguards with me. I was very precious to them, don't you know!"

"Like me. I'm precious!" Mimi piped up.

"Don't interrupt," said Uncle, holding up a paw in the darkness.

"Why did you need bodyguards?" asked Little Dream.

"Ah, because of the *dangers!*" said Uncle. "Because of the enemies that lurk in every hollow in the sand and under every thorn bush!"

"Oh dear," sighed Little Dream.

"Don't forget The Silent Enemy in the sky," added Mimi, who liked to show how clever she was. Uncle gave a trembling twitch and a gasp and she got a sharp nudge in the ribs from Skeema. "Sorry, Uncle!" she exclaimed. "I didn't mean to upset you."

Uncle Fearless took another deep breath to pull himself together. "N-never mind. No harm done," he murmured. It took him a while to calm down, but pretty soon he was happily showing off again. "As I have often told you, it is the meerkat way to stand by one another," he said. "But your old Uncle was not afraid. Oh no, I was young and keen! I said to my subjects, I said: 'I am the greatest of all the Sharpeyes! Do you imagine that I am not brave enough or wise enough to explore my own kingdom *by myself* from time to time if I wish?' And so I ventured out alone, something that you kits must never, *never* do. Soon I had marked every corner where a kat can sniff! I discovered all there was to know out there among the sizzlingly hot Salt Pans at the far end of the kingdom. And do you know the most interesting thing that I discovered?"

"The pointy mounds!" cried the kits together. They liked this bit. "Where the funny Blah-blahs live… **IN THE AIR ABOVE THE GROUND**!"

"Exactly!" cried Uncle. "The Blah-blahs build hollow, pointy mounds, quite close together on TOP of the sand, what-what! Each mound is a burrow for a small tribe. Each mound is taller than a thorn tree; pointy at the top and much wider at the bottom. And do you know," Uncle went on, letting them into the secret, "there's no strength in those mounds at all. The walls are so thin that they ripple in the wind! Isn't that ridiculous? A jackal could tear through those walls in two bites!"

"Ah, but the Blah-blahs are bigger and stronger than us, aren't they, Uncle Fearless?" put in Skeema.

"Oh, yes!" said Uncle. "They're giants. But in many ways they are just like us, only much funnier – and MUCH more charming and cute. I came across several tribes in my travels. Now, who do you want me to tell you about? The Oolooks

21

who always jump up and down when they see a rhino or a giraffe and call *oolook-oolook!* Or would you like to hear about the Whevubins that are always dashing about calling *hurryupp-hurryupp!* when they can't find their young. And when they do find them again, they chase them up and down calling *whevubin- whevubin!*

Little Dream took his thumb out of his mouth and said wetly, "Click-clicks. Say about you and the Click-clicks."

Uncle scratched his ear with his back leg and he shook so violently that the kits had to hang on tight so as not to fall off his lap. The two biggest ones clung to his chest hair and Little Dream had to keep a good grip on the collar Uncle always wore with great pride.

"Well then, Little Dream," he said. "This collar you can feel round my neck was presented to me as a mark of respect by a very important

Blah-blah. He was Chief of the Click-click tribe, no less! I used to see him passing by every day in his Vroom-vroom."

"What's a Vroom-vroom?" asked Mimi.

"Vroom-vrooms are huge, dreadful things!" said Uncle. "How can I explain? Ah, yes… now you all know that meerkats always make sure to dig plenty of escape tunnels when we build a burrow, don't you?" (He felt his little audience nodding away.) "Well, the flimsy mounds where the Blah-blahs live have only one entrance. So they keep special moving burrows nearby and jump into them whenever they sense danger. At the first sign of a lion or a rhino or any animal that bites or tramples – off they run, *Vroom-vroom*! Those things can move like stampeding wildebeest, what-what!"

"Oh, really, Uncle!" laughed Skeema not believing a word, but still enjoying the story.

"You'll be telling us next that Vroom-vrooms have got legs!"

"Not at all, my boy. They glide along on round spinners that throw up clouds of sand, so they do! They do a terrible amount of roaring and dust-kicking and sometimes they let out an alarm call… *Barp-barp!* I'm pretty certain that these are tricks to frighten their enemies. But did your Uncle Fearless jump down the nearest bolthole when he saw them coming?"

24

"Never! No way!" cheered the kits.

"Of course not!" crowed Uncle Fearless. "I stood my ground like a king…"

"And then you *tamed* Chief Click-click!" cried Little Dream, full of admiration.

Skeema rolled his eyes. *It's all made up*, he thought. Still, he didn't want to interrupt a good yarn.

"Well done, Dreamie! Yes, I tamed him. Mind you, it took ages before he and two of his subjects plucked up the courage to leave the safety of their Vroom-vroom. But finally they came out. And bit by bit they moved closer towards me on their tall, tall hind legs. The Chief led the way. He was very shy in spite of his great bigness and at first he only dared look at me through the shiny box he held up in front of his eyes to protect them!

Sometimes the chief went *click-click!* with his tongue, too, meaning that he was my subject. As each suntime passed, he became bolder and moved a little closer, bringing me tasty gifts of food. In the end he knelt on the sand in front of me and bowed down – completely tame. "You are my king!" he seemed to say. I could do what I wanted with him. He even allowed me to climb on to his head and use him as a look-out post."

"Oo! What did he feel like?" gasped Little Dream. "Are they furry like us?"

"Well, let me tell you… When you climb up any of the Blah-blahs you will find that their legs are mostly smooth and warm. They feel dry like bark. Yet on the middle parts of their bodies they have a covering. It's soft, I would say, not at all furry. Except on their heads. A lot of them have fur on their heads."

"Uncle! Have you *really* climbed a Blah-blah?" said Mimi.

"Oh, many times! Once they know who's boss they're safe as burrows to be with."

"What did the other Sharpeyes say when you told them?" asked Skeema, giggling. "Did they say, 'Oo, Your Majesty! What a big fibber you are! There's no such things as Blah-blahs or galloping Vroom-vrooms! You're just making this all up…'?"

27

He got a nip for being cheeky, but only a play-bite. Uncle was very fond of him. "Not at all, you saucy young dung beetle!" he boomed. "Most of the tribe were too scared to come out of the burrow at first, but when at last they did, they saw for themselves. Of course, it took a bit of time to get used to the size of the great clumsy creatures, but in the end all the Sharpeyes got to know them. In fact, we did our best to teach the Blah-blahs useful skills. We showed them the way to dig proper burrows, how to forage for food, how to do sentry duty… all that sort of thing. We even showed them how to do a war dance. The sad thing was, the Click-clicks turned out to be a bit stupid. They never did anything much, apart from sitting and hiding behind their eye-protectors."

"I believe all of it," said Little Dream. He never doubted his dear old babysitter.

"Mind you," added Uncle a little sadly, "all this was… Harrumph! …before my… er… accident, of course. I couldn't be a king any more after that. My brother had to take my place."

"Sad," murmured Little Dream.

Suddenly Uncle's fur stood stiff and he was on the alert. "Wup-wup-wup!" he called urgently, and pulled the kits tighter to him.

"What is it, Uncle?" whispered Skeema.

"I can feel something! There! The ground's shaking!" said Mimi.

Loose sand began to drift on to them from the ceiling. The kits began to cough and whimper.

"Is it an enemy?" whispered Little Dream. Skeema jumped down from Uncle's lap and darted round the chamber making spit-noises. He always liked to have a plan. His present one was to run to an escape tunnel. He found himself digging furiously at the chamber door to get out.

"It's an earthquake, possibly," said Uncle. "Hush, now, Skeema. Stay with the group."

"*Vroom-vroom!*" breathed Little Dream.

Chapter 2

After a minute or two, it was silent once more.
Uncle sounded the all-clear – *Yee-oh-oo-oo-oo!* –
then he mused, "Do you know, Little Dream, you
may have been right. I suppose it *could* have been
a Vroom-vroom." He paused to have a sniff and a
think. "But I doubt it. They *never* come over to this
side of the kingdom of the Sharpeyes. No." He
clacked his teeth together to show that he had
made up his mind. "I think it much more likely
that the sandstorm was playing tricks in the
tunnels."

The kits relaxed. As soon as the danger passed they were asking questions about the Blah-blahs again.

"Do they stand on all fours?" Mimi wanted to know.

And Little Dream asked: "Why they want to hide their eyes all the time?"

"Ha-ha! Good questions! To answer yours first, Mimi: mostly they seem to move on their hind legs. And, as I mentioned before, they're taller than ant hills. Do you remember our lesson, where I taught you all how to stand like sentries?"

"Yes, yes," squeaked the cubs, wriggling and stretching out their hind legs.

"Well that's how the Blah-blahs stand!"

"I can stand!" squealed Little Dream and showed them. It was too dark to see him struggling to balance. Finally he fell on his nose. *Bonk!* The others heard him, but took no notice.

"Do you mean the *she*-Blah-blahs as well as the *he*-Blah-blahs?" Mimi squeaked. "Can the she-Blah-blahs stand? Like Mimi? Like me? Like me?"

"Oh, give yourself a rest!" said Skeema scornfully.

"Yes, Mimi, hush now," said Uncle Fearless. "The Chief of the Click-clicks always has a female with him. Her legs are as long as the trunks of young baobab trees. She has a long, pale mane but no fur otherwise and she has longer claws than the male. Sometimes they shine bright like red berries. Her calls are softer than the males except her alarm calls. Oh my goodness, I remember once when a scorpion scooted right up to her paw! She could easily have pounced on it and sucked the juice out of it. But what did she do? She did a funny sort of war dance and ran away making a noise like a scared baboon – *eee!-eee!-eee!*"

Skeema enjoyed that. "Now make up something funny about the males," he begged.

"He's *not* making it up," insisted Little Dream.

"Ah, yes, I was going to tell Dreamie about their eyes, wasn't I?" said Uncle, ignoring Skeema. "The Blah-blahs look rather like meerkat kits in a way, because their eyes are dark and usually on the front of their faces, but they're flat and square and very shiny."

"What do you mean, *usually on the front?*" asked Skeema. "Can they move them to other parts of their face?"

"Oh, yes. Their eyes are joined to their ears by little arms. So sometimes the Blah-blahs lift their eyes up and put them on top of their heads."

"Oh!" gasped Mimi.

"Oh, yes, they're very strange," said Uncle. "The Blah-blahs' noses are quite small compared to ours, so perhaps they can't smell very well and they depend on their eyes to keep them safe. Their eyes are so dark and shiny that when I first got close to the Chief and he was sitting down I thought I was looking at a mighty meerkat warrior from a rival tribe! It took me quite a while to realise that I was looking at myself!"

"Vrrrrr!" purred the kits, though not all of them quite believed this part.

"Now, now, it's getting late," said Uncle. "We must all get plenty of sleep. We have a big day ahead tomorrow, remember!"

"Oh, please," begged Mimi. "Tell me just one little bit more."

"Just two things," put in Skeema.

"Oh, all right. I'll just tell you one or two more

things that made us Sharpeyes chuckle and that's *all*. I'll start with one of the Chief's bodyguards.

Sometimes he carried a tiny spear and shield with him. I don't know what he was thinking of. It was far too small to protect anyone! And he spent hours squatting down, just scratching the shield with the point of the spear. Very odd! And instead of marking out his territory in the normal way by squirting things with his scent glands, he…"

"He *what*, Uncle?"

"Now you *are* going to think I'm telling you a whopper. Every now and then he put a small white stick in his mouth and set fire to it! Then he blew smoke out of his nose. Honestly! He looked like a warthog snuffling about on a frosty morning!"

The kits kicked their little legs and laughed till tears ran down their faces. It made Uncle laugh just to listen to them. "Honestly-hee-hee!" he protested. "I'm not making this up! Oh, I can't wait to lead you up into the sunlight and get your eyes working! I'll teach you trees! Colours! Sky! Dry white sand, rich wet sand after the rains! You'll see how a tasty scorpion dances when it's cornered! I'll teach you how to rub the stink-juice off a millipede by dragging it across the sand! Believe me, seeing is almost as much fun as smelling, what-what! Hang on! I must just have another scratch."

"Look out everyone! Here comes another earthquake!" giggled Skeema.

"Help! A flea-storm!" squealed Mimi with a chuckle.

Uncle pretended to have a fierce fight with them – which was just what they wanted. They rolled about the chamber for a while, wrestling and yipping and play-snarling and snapping.

"Oof! That's enough! You've quite worn me out!" puffed Uncle, dusting himself down.

"Uncle! Is it easy to climb a Blah-blah?" asked Mimi, wanting more, as usual.

"Oh, easy as sneezing! I remember one time I was…" Suddenly he was alert and on his back feet again, shaking the kits on to the floor. "There! You almost got me started again!" he said with a laugh. "But it's *way* past your bedtime."

He rolled the kits into a bundle and stood over them in the guard position, growling gently but firmly. "No more talk. Busy day tomorrow. There are *so* many lessons for you to learn, you're going to need all your strength."

Chapter 3

The pups were very excited and also rather nervous. Still, they slept soundly.

Fearless was not so lucky. He was troubled by his usual nightmare. He dreamed of beaks and claws and fighting and falling. He flung out his arms and legs like a star! This always happened just at the moment when a giant eagle owl dropped him and left him falling towards the rocks. His jerking and kicking and shouts of terror shocked him awake – and woke everyone else.

Little Dream was the first to comfort him. "Safe, Uncle," he said and held him tight. He groomed him for a moment, feeling through his fur for fleas. As soon as Skeema and Mimi had their wits about them, they were up and hugging him, too.

"I don't know what all this fuss is about," grumbled Uncle, trying to pretend nothing had happened, but trembling all the same.

"If The Silent Enemy comes down on us when we reach the Upworld, I'm going to bite his head off!" said Skeema, doing his best to sound brave.

"Good lad!" said Uncle. "That's the spirit! But don't you worry about enemies. We shall be perfectly safe so long as we look out for one another. You see, I was... well, I was on my own. I was caught off guard, what-what! It was hunger that did it. My mind was on a tasty rock lizard, d'you see? The eagle owl saw his chance, came out of the sun, snatched me into the air and took out my eye with his claw."

"Poor Uncle," said Little Dream.

"Never be off your guard!" warned Uncle. His voice grew stronger as he added: "Ah! But at least I gave him a taste of his own medicine! I pulled a great mouthful of feathers out of his chest! Ha-ha! That shook him! That showed him who was boss! He couldn't hold me then, what-what!"

He decided not to mention that the eagle owl had dropped him from a great height and smashed several of his bones. This was not the time. He took a deep breath to stop himself from shaking at the memory of it. "But it was all rather a shock, I don't mind telling you. It took

me a very long time to get my strength back,"
he went on. "My mind wandered. I was feverish!
I was weak as a grub! The rest of the Sharpeyes
thought I had the Meerkat Madness. They
didn't think I'd live. So naturally, they had to
choose another…"

He couldn't bring himself to finish the
sentence and so Little Dream said, "Never
mind. You can be our secret king."

"Hear, hear!" cried Skeema and Mimi.
"Three cheers for our secret king!"

"Harrumph!" grunted Uncle, feeling foolish.
"No more nonsense, now! Up and follow, kits.
Up and follow." Without another word he
began digging at the nursery door.

The kits had learned their lessons well and
stood in line behind him in their digging order.
Each passed the scooped-out sand to the one
behind, as if they were passing buckets of water

to put out a fire. Skeema was right behind
Uncle Fearless, his brave heart pounding; then
Mimi, then Little Dream. In a flash they had
removed more sand than they all weighed
together – and found themselves in a damp and
chilly passageway.

Blindly they followed their noses and ears
through this and other passages and into a
wider space. Uncle told them in a whisper that
they had reached the main tunnel. There were
strange new smells in each place they came to –
of pee and dung that was not theirs – and the
kits' paws were tickled by unknown dung beetles
at work with their loads.

"On," said Uncle. "And say nothing
until I tell you."

They followed silently until the tunnel did a
peculiar thing. Its blackness rolled back and
became something else, not so solid. This made

them gasp and Dream began to whimper quietly.

"Don't worry. This is just the sunlight pushing in," said Uncle. "It creeps into the burrow slowly so as not to shock our eyes. You'll notice it grow bigger as we get closer to the Upworld. But it won't harm us. It'll warm us up and make us feel quick and tricky. Then you will understand what we call 'seeing'. You'll enjoy it once you're used to it."

They pressed forward and smelled new air as the darkness began to move aside for a stronger kind of light that made the kits' eyes blink. It was there in the half-darkness that Chancer surprised them. His smell slid out of a side-tunnel first. Then came his slick head. That was finally followed by the swaying body of the King of the Sharpeyes himself.

"Welcome to the Upworld, brother Fearless!" said Chancer. He didn't *sound* very welcoming. "The Queen's hungry," he went on. "She's keen to forage on the hunting grounds, but she is waiting to greet the young ones at the entrance to the burrow. So hurry. Come this way. "

Chapter 4

Queen Heartless was nibbling a grasshopper when Fragrant's kits and their babysitter were bundled into her presence. She was waiting on The Spoil, the loose sand heaped up just in front of the main entrance. Fearless had once been her husband but after his 'accident' with The Silent Enemy she had taken Chancer, Fearless's younger brother, as her new husband. Chancer ruled the Sharpeyes with Queen Heartless now. He was the father of her royal kits.

So Queen Heartless hardly glanced at Fearless.

He meant nothing to her any more. That was the meerkat way. It was something he simply had to accept. Still, if it was painful for him to be no more than a babysitter, he did his best not to show it.

The Queen puffed up her fine pale fur and sat up proudly, staring into the sun. Her back was to the newcomers as they crept, blinking, out of the burrow. The royal kits, Princes Spiteful, Needleclaw and Snatch stood beside her with Princess Dangerous. A little way off the rest of the tribe stood to attention or bobbed busily, scanning the skies and the sands all around for enemies.

The sun was still low in the sky, so the eyes of Skeema, Mimi and Little Dream were dazzled. Their first sight in this amazing new Upworld was of something shockingly bright and yellow-orange.

47

*

For a second, poor Little Dream thought that the Queen must be the sun itself. It hurt his eyes to look at her and he had to turn away. Most meerkats have dark patches round their deep-set eyes that allow them to look directly into the sun without damage to their sight. Not so, Little Dream. He was born with eye-patches that were so pale they could hardly be seen at all. The royal family were quick to notice this and Princess Dangerous could not stop herself from giggling. "Look at that one! Have you ever *seen* such silly eyes!" she whispered.

Skeema and Mimi looked dazed. They felt weak and chilly. Uncle had told them about the need to warm up their tummy-pads by standing in the sunshine and they tried to stand to attention as they knew they had to. Unfortunately, the journey through the tunnels had made them very

tired and they wobbled and fell over. There was
more laughter, this time from Prince Needleclaw.

The queen stopped nibbling for a moment. The
grasshopper was still wriggling although she had
just chewed its head off. "Have the new kits been
marked?" she asked the King.

"Stand still," ordered King Chancer and sprayed
them with the royal smell.

FFFT-
            FFFT-
                        FFFT!

Queen Heartless-the-Dazzling looked down her
long and elegant nose at her damp new subjects.
   "*Now you share our Sharpeyes' burrow,*" she
announced coldly.

Now you share our Sharpeyes' smell.

Now and forever you are Sharpeyes!

"Repeat after me the Sharpeye motto: *Stay alert to stay alive. And stay with the group.*"

"*Stay alert to stay alive,*" repeated Skeema, Mimi and Little Dream. "*And stay with the group.*"

"You may now bow and scrape."

The kits copied Uncle Fearless as he bowed and scraped and licked the royal face and fur, the Queen's first, then the King's. "Now you must greet the princes and the princess," whispered Uncle. It turned out that the royal kits didn't want to be licked. Instead, they formed a noisy gang and rolled the visitors over. Since they were much larger than Skeema, Mimi and Little Dream, they could do it easily. They went for Skeema first, snapping and snarling and turning him on his back in the hot sand. This caught Skeema completely by surprise. Still, he began to give as good as he got, returning with interest the bites and scratches he was given.

Uncle Fearless managed to get in among the scrapping bodies and whisper into his ear: "Give way, Skeema! Remember your place!"

Then it was Mimi's turn to be knocked about, and finally, Little Dream's. Mimi was nipped quite sharply but did her best to be brave and not make a fuss. Apart from Uncle, not one of the rest of the watching Sharpeyes moved or said a word.

When the royal kits turned on Little Dream he let out a warning call and words started to tumble out of him: "*Wup-wup-wup*! Don't you pick on me or you'll upset Bold Uncle Fearless and he doesn't like bad manners and he's our secret king and once he bit The Silent Enemy!"

"How dare you speak to us like that!" spluttered Princess Dangerous.

Little Dream took no notice. "*And* he is the King of the Click-clicks!" he went on. "And he's not scared of Vroom-vrooms, and he can stand on a Blah-blah's head, so you be careful!" It was the longest speech he had ever made.

A dreadful hush fell. This was unheard of! A kit – a commoner kit at that – speaking up without an invitation! In front of Her Majesty! Some of the humbler Sharpeyes began to murmur.

"Who does that kit think he is?"

"He must be mad!"

"It's all that Fearless's fault, putting ideas into his head! Secret king, indeed!"

"Yes, because he had The Madness himself – remember?"

"You're right! Do you remember the time, just after the eagle owl attacked him and dropped him on his head? He twitched, he was helpless... he talked rubbish, poor kat."

"Such a shame!"

The Queen silenced them all with a sharp cry. Nobody moved. She returned for a moment to her grasshopper, snapping off the legs one by one. For a moment there was no other sound except the whirring of insect wings. Then she said, "I have no time for any more nonsense. Tell me, Fearless, are you or any of these kits likely to be a danger to me or to my tribe?"

"N-n-not at all, Your Majesty." Fearless was flustered but trying to seem steady.

"A babysitter's job is to mind babies," she said. "Not to fill their heads with nonsense. Mind them. Teach them how to be useful and how to obey. Anything else is… unwelcome. Do you understand?"

"Absolutely, Your Majesty. I—"

"Chancer, children, come!" she interrupted. "I lost more weight in the darktime than is good for me. I must forage for food without delay."

With that, she turned and galloped off towards the hunting grounds.

Chapter 5

"I say, look here, my dear young Dreamer," said Uncle as they stood alone by the burrow entrance on the very edge of the Upworld. "You mustn't go about saying that I'm your... your actual *king*. I mean it's awfully kind of you but it's just not done."

"Ah, but we *like* you being our king," said Little Dream. Small flurries of hot sand blown on the wind made him stagger and squint. Luckily nature had fitted him with little wind screen wipers, so the sand in his eyes was quickly flicked away.

"It was supposed to be a *secret*, Dreamie, you bedbug! You're not supposed to tell anybody secrets!" scolded Skeema. He turned to Uncle, who was looking ruffled and uncomfortable. "Don't worry, we won't *say* you're our king out loud, we'll just know it," he assured him, anxious to make him feel better about himself.

"Hear, hear!" said Mimi. "You can keep being my secret king too. Now could you be quick and teach me the Warm-up, pleeeeease. I'm freezing!"

Uncle Fearless looked at his loyal, brave and shivering secret subjects and his one eye filled with tears.

"Harrrrumph!" he said, wiping them away with the back of his paw. "No more nonsense. Stand by me and watch carefully. This is how we Sharpeyes do the Warm-up. It's very important that you get it right. Meerkats lose a lot of their strength keeping warm in the burrow in the darktime.

When we come up here at suntime, we need to forage and to feed. To forage well, we need to be quick and tricky. And to be quick and tricky we do – *this*. Hup*!*" He put his front paws under his big fat tummy and heaved up his black tummy-pad so that it soaked up the sun's rays.

"Hup!" giggled Skeema, Mimi and Little Dream, pretending that they had big fat tummies to pull up and falling flat on their backs.

"Quiet, you saucy young tics!" roared Uncle, pretending to be furious. "Warm up properly or you won't get any breakfast!"

The kits' first foraging trip in the Upworld was so exciting that Skeema and Mimi completely forgot about the coldness of King Chancer and Queen Heartless and their horrid, spoilt, royal kits. They were out of sight of the burrow by the Grove of the Prickly Shrubs. The late summer rains had caused grasses and bright, sweet-smelling flowers to shoot everywhere, but they didn't notice. They had food on their minds.

Uncle showed them how to sniff for damp sand under the hot dry top-sand. This was where delicious snacks crawled and tunnelled, just asking to be dug out and snapped up. Skeema and Mimi worked a little apart from each other, scrabbling with their front paws and heaving up a mound of sand behind them as if they'd done it all their lives. They found larvae and beetles a plenty. It was terribly exciting, like finding buried treasure, and their squeaks and chatter filled the morning air. Even so, they understood that they were never to get so excited as to have both their heads down at once. While one was digging, the other had to look around for danger.

If the bigger kits were quick learners, Little Dream wasn't quite so confident. Uncle fed him a couple of sandworms to keep him going and then took him a little way away up the slope of a sand dune, through the Whispering Grasses until they were standing not far from Leaning Camelthorn. Suddenly Little Dream dropped flat. "Enemies!" he hissed.

"Don't worry," Uncle told him. "Those are eland. They just feed on grass – oh, and those really big ones? Those are blue wildebeest. They won't hurt you either, not unless they stand on you. Come on. I'm going to show you High Guarding."

Patiently he nursed the nervous little kit up the leaning trunk of the ancient tree and on to the branch above. "Keep going," he urged. Up they went to the next branch, then the next. "Look down there and you can see Skeema and Mimi on The Spoil, by the birth-burrow entrance. Yes? Now look right over there. You see those hills where the sky ends? Somewhere on the other side of them is Far Burrow. Now turn this way. Can you see Bolthole Sands where the rest of the tribe is foraging? There are plenty of places to run to if an enemy comes, what-what! Now, look at those trees just beyond. What do you see?"

He was pointing to a small forest of black thorns. Some of them had grown into quite tall trees. A few vultures had gathered in a line on the lower branches. Right at the top, a martial eagle was gazing about.

"Don't worry about the droopy ones, the vultures," whispered Uncle. "But keep an eye on that eagle. He's one of our worst enem—" And that was when Little Dream fell off his perch.

Uncle climbed down, checked him over, helped him up to his post and got him settled. The wind blew, just a little bit. Little Dream's branch swayed, just a little bit.

He fell off.

He climbed up. He wobbled.

He fell off.

Luckily he fell into soft sand every time, so he wasn't hurt at all and Uncle kept encouraging him. "Up. Straighten your back! Tail stiff and steady. That's it! Now – paws together. Bravo! You've got it, laddie!'" he called.

Little Dream wobbled. Tail up… Miracle! He clung on. At last – hooray!

"Well done," said Uncle. "Now, let's practise our calls. Remember to keep chirping the all-clear if there's no danger. Off you go, if you can remember it."

"Um, is it *Ee-oo-oo Ooo-oo-oo?*" asked Little Dream timidly.

61

"That'll do nicely," said Uncle. "Keep it up. And keep watching all around because I've only got the one eye, what-what?"

Mimi had almost disappeared under the sand to the side of The Spoil and suddenly she was up on the surface, tossing something in her paws. "Look! I've caught something, Uncle! Aren't I clever? What *is* this? Wheee! It's so wiggly! But I'm even more wiggly! Look!"

"Oh, do stop showing off," came Skeema's growly voice. "Just eat the thing."

Mimi pulled a face but she was too hungry to argue with her brother. She tucked into her snack instead and planned to get him back later.

"Well done, Mimi. You're learning. There's a time to snap and a time to chew. Looks like you've found yourself a gecko," called Uncle. "Eat it up. Geckos have very juicy eyeballs. Yum-yum!"

The thought of something so delicious was too

much for Little Dream who was feeling rather peckish himself. "*Yyippp!-Yyippp! Yyippp!-Yyippp!*" he yelled.

Uncle Fearless stiffened and then immediately scampered among the branches like a frantic squirrel. "ACTION STATIONS!" he shrieked. "AIR ATTACK! EAGLE OWL COMING IN! BOLTHOLE! BOLTHOLE! RUN-RUN-RUN!"

He knocked Little Dream off his perch, got behind him as soon as he hit the sand, bit his bottom, shoved him along with his nose and zipped after Skeema and Mimi who were both running in circles on the sand.

"DON'T PANIC!" Uncle yelled (though there was a touch of panic in his voice). "GO LEFT! LEFT! NOT THAT WAY! BY THE ROCK! THAT'S IT! DIVE-DIVE-DIVE!" And down the bolthole everyone darted at last.

They panted. Held their breath together to

listen. Panted. Couldn't hear anything. Peeped out. Couldn't see anything. Panted. No sign of a single bird in the wide blue sky, let alone an eagle owl!

"I can't see any sign of danger, Dreamer, old son. What was it you spotted?"

"Um, I didn't spot anything," muttered Little Dream "You said about gecko eyeballs. I got excited."

"What? I... You... got EXCITED?!" spluttered Uncle. "But you were on guard, laddie! You were our eyes and ears! You mustn't sound the Eagle-Owl Alarm every time you get a bit peckish! You nearly gave me a heart attack."

"Nit wit!" complained Skeema. "You know eagle owls make Uncle panic!"

"Panic? Me? I wasn't panicking!" blustered Uncle.

"You made me drop my gecko!" moaned Mimi.

"Right, you two!" growled Uncle. "You can jolly well be quiet! You didn't put on much of a show yourselves just now! Dashing about in circles like a couple of bushbabies! What did I tell you? Always check for a bolthole *before* you get your heads down."

Skeema could see how much his careless words had upset Uncle Fearless. When he remembered how much damage the beak and claw of an eagle owl had done to him, he felt ashamed of himself. He went over and rolled at Uncle's feet to show he was sorry.

Uncle accepted the apology. Then he noticed that all the kits were looking crestfallen. "Ah, now look here. Come on, chirp up, everyone. We're all still alive, aren't we? We've learnt a few more survival skills, what-what! All good experience. Well done. Perfect! Just remember, now: *'Danger up and danger down. Clever kits check all around!'*

Everyone got that? Good. Breakfast here we come!"

"Whirrrr-wee-ooo!" cried the kits with enthusiasm. Up went the rusty tip of Uncle's tail. It waved like a flag and led them off like lightning back to their hunting ground.

Chapter 6

The next suntime the kits stood with the rest of
the tribe at Warm-up and they all did it very well.
Secretly Mimi and Skeema hoped for a word of
praise from the King or Queen but they got
nothing but a squirt from King Chancer and icy
looks from Queen Heartless. The royal kits were
positively rude. They said they were of no
importance at all. They called them babies and
tenderpaws.

Once again the whole tribe dashed off to the
hunting grounds, leaving Uncle Fearless to teach

his group their lessons by themselves near the entrance to the burrow. He decided to give Skeema and Mimi some look-out practice, so off they raced to Leaning Camelthorn and scampered to the top. Meanwhile he took Little Dream a little way beyond The Spoil to demonstrate some of the finer points of foraging.

Little Dream sniffed at the hot dry white sand.

"The food worth a chase

Lives in a damp place," he said, repeating one of Uncle's lessons.

"Quite right. And where's the dampness? Under the surface, yes? Well, come on, young scrabbler, get your claws into it! You must be hungry."

Little Dream *was* hungry and he dug as hard as he could. The soft white sand flew like dust and soon his paw-pads felt the cool, moist, yellower stuff underneath. Uncle's head bobbed up and down to make sure that no four-legged enemy surprised them. "Keep contact! Keep calling!" he told Skeema and Mimi who were doing a nice job up the tree. Soon Little Dream dug out his first creepy-crawly and tucked in. He loved the way it tickled going down. Ahhh! He smacked his lips. He felt stronger already. In went his digging claws.

"Did I ever tell you about the time the tribe was surrounded by Ruddertail warriors, out on the Plain of the Antelopes?" began Uncle.

Little Dream dug away, too interested in finding food to listen.

"Dashed big meerkats, they were, with eee-NOR-mously long tails," Uncle continued, as if Little Dream were fascinated. "Turned on us, they did! They outnumbered us three to one! The brutes thought they could take over one of our best boltholes. You should have heard their war cries. And the teeth on them! Yet we Sharpeyes

69

stood firm. I remember, I got up
on a mound, a tall ant hill it was… or was it a
shepherd tree? Aghhh! – can't quite remember.
Anyway, whatever it was, I got up it. Frightfully
high, it was. I let out a war cry of my own…"

Up in the branches of the Camelthorn tree,
without taking her eyes off the skies for a moment,
Mimi giggled and whispered to Skeema. "Listen to
Uncle," she whispered. "He's on about his Glory
Days again!"

"I'm sure he makes it all up!" whispered
Skeema.

Uncle's voice grew louder. "…so I said to my
troops, I said, 'Tails up for King Fearless, my lads
and lasses! Show 'em your teeth and show 'em the
Sharpeye WAR DANCE!'"

Uncle was getting really excited now. He sang
and he danced, jumping up and down on his hind
legs, head up, fur bristling, showing his fine yellow

teeth. "The Chief of the Click-clicks was *very* impressed by this one too, I can tell you!" he said, really getting into it. "Oh, yes. I remember him watching me and the rest of the tribe chasing away a puff adder! He was *terrified*! He stood still as a stick hoping his eye-protectors would keep him safe, the silly great termite heap!" Soon Uncle was wobbling his bottom about and trying to remember some of the trickier steps. "Now, let me see, how did it go?

"*Bouncy-bouncy!*
Boom-boom! Call!
Stand-up! Tail-up!
Make-yourself-tall!
Head-butt! Head-butt!
Strike like a snake!
Spit-spit-spit-spit!
Shaky-shake-SHAKE!"

Mimi and Skeema nearly fell off their branches, laughing.

Luckily, Uncle Fearless didn't notice, because just at that moment, Little Dream uncovered his first – very angry, very poisonous – scorpion.

"Wh… wh… what do I do?" squeaked Little Dream.

"Bravo, my young hunter!" he exclaimed. "You've hit the jackpot! And talking of war dances – here's a chap with a very interesting dance of his own, what-what!"

Little Dream peered closely as the scorpion turned his back on him.

"Watch out!" warned Uncle. "He'll have you with that big sting on his tail if you're not quick and tricky!"

Too late! The scorpion moved like lightning. It did a scuffling little shimmy, turned its back and brought his nasty curved claw down right on to

72

Little Dream's tender nose!

"Yow! He bit me!" screamed Little Dream.

"Then get after him and bite him back!" roared Uncle.

Skeema and Mimi saw what was happening and started screeching. "Eee-eee! He's going to die!" they cried from above. "Help him, Uncle!"

"Stay at your posts, keep the all-clear sounding and keep a sharp look-out!" barked Uncle. "Let our Dreamer alone to learn the scorpion dance. Come on, Little Dream, back-and-forth, back-and-forth and dodge his sting. Now go for him! Snap his tail off before he stings you again."

Little Dream rubbed his nose and looked at the angry scorpion. It skipped, skidded round like a mad little bumper car, skipped sideways, backwards, forwards, all the time waving its poisoned weapon.

"You're all right! He can give you a nasty nip

73

but his poison can't kill a meerkat," Uncle told Little Dream. "Get after him. Quick and tricky wins the game!"

Little Dream began to growl, "Krrrr-Krrr!" He watched the scorpion closely. When he got close, the scorpion struck. This time it missed. "Ha-ha!" cried Little Dream. He moved in – and back. He stepped sideways – dodged the sting – stepped back. Forward. Missed! "Look! Watch me dancing!" cried Little Dream. And when the scorpion lunged at his nose once more, he bit off the sting, grabbed its body in his jaws and took a big juicy bite. "Mmmm!" he murmured. "Yummy!"

It was the most delicious thing he'd ever tasted.

High overhead, too high just now to dive and strike, The Silent Enemy circled and noted what was going on. He could feel the tightness of the wound in his chest. The scar left by a shocking bite from the very meerkat he was watching had spoiled the perfect smoothness of his feathers. Some lifted like porcupine bristles where they should have lain smoothly.

Fearless stiffened and shuddered as he heard the distant, mocking hoots of the eagle owl. "*Hoo-hoo yu-hu-hu-hoooh!*" He guessed what they meant. "You just wait! You will pay for what you-hoo-hoo did to me-he-he! I'll have your other eye-hi-hi!"

Chapter 7

The kits continued to work very hard at their
studies. By their third suntime in the Upworld
they could all do Warm-up without wobbling or
falling over, even Little Dream. They were much
better at high and low guarding and foraging for
themselves. They got better at grooming and
searching one another for tics and fleas, and they
had learned to defend themselves from the surprise
play-attacks of older pups. They looked like
Sharpeyes, the king made sure they smelled like
Sharpeyes, but they still didn't really feel that

they were wanted by the rest of the tribe.

Skeema was bored. He was anxious to get away from the entrance to the burrow and do some exploring far away. "When are we going to have some adventures like you, Uncle?" he kept asking impatiently.

"Oh, soon," Fearless said in a vague sort of way. "Once you've learned all the ways of the tribe."

"Bor-ing!" muttered Skeema under his breath.

By now they had wandered over to a dune of dazzling white sand. It was steep and towered over them like a great wave. It must have been formed by the sandstorm that they had heard while they were still living in the nursery chamber. Its side felt hot even to padded little feet and so soft that it ran down like water at the least disturbance. Playfully, Little Dream began to burrow, pulling away like mad with his front paws.

"Pack it in!" cried Skeema, turning his bad

temper on him.

"Don't be so silly, Dreamie!" snapped Mimi, joining in. "There's nothing in there. It's much too dry for foraging!"

"*You* say, Uncle!" said Little Dream. "*You* say, *No, my subject! Stand still, I command you! Obey your king! Stop that digging or you will feel the points of my teeth!*"

Uncle couldn't help smiling just a little. "Now look here, Dreamie, old chap," he said. "Be sensible and, er, let's all trot along and find a bit of shade. It's much too hot to…"

He noticed that Little Dream had stopped listening and was digging more frantically if anything. "Come along, now, Little Dream!" Uncle said. "We mustn't stay out in the open too long. Do as I say, now. Seriously, this is a command. I'm ordering you now…"

Little Dream's head came up for air. "I can

smell something!" he panted excitedly.

"Leave it, Dreamie," said Uncle. "There's a good kit."

"Something big," said Little Dream. "Look!"

At first, just a corner of the something came to light. It was shiny pink and had a hard shell. Little Dream's sharp claws could only skid over the surface of it, making a hollow sound.

"Hey! Dreamer's found a tortoise!" said Mimi, excitedly. "Let Mimi help you! Me! me!"

She tried to barge Skeema out of the way but he was eager to dig too. So was Uncle Fearless. It was time to use his king voice. "Stand back!" he commanded.

Instantly, the kits obeyed. "Stand guard!" he ordered. They stood to attention, glancing about like the Old Guard. Uncle took a deep breath and hauled sand like the master-digger he was. "If it's a tortoise, it's the biggest one I've ever seen, what-what!" he puffed, as he kept digging. "I need help here. Bob and dig, bob and dig!"

"Aye, aye, Your Majesty!" said Little Dream. This was just the way he wanted life to be.

Many claws make light work and in no time at all, whatever it was lay big and oblong and pink and strange and sideways on the stony sand.

"Is it just a big shell, Uncle?" asked Mimi. "Or do we have to turn it over to get at the meat?" She brushed accidentally against one of the round spinners on its feet which made a dull whirring sound as it whizzed round. She yelped and jumped back!

She couldn't help it. She let out the general alarm call: "Wai-wow-wik-wak!"

Skeema laughed. "Don't make such a fuss, Mimi!" he scoffed. "It won't trample you. It's not really an elephant, is it, Uncle?"

Little Dream placed a paw on the shell. His eyes were shining. "Vrrroom-vroom!" he said.

Chapter 8

Uncle stalked gravely round the large pink object that Little Dream had discovered. His nose and his one eye got busy.

"Hmmm. Look at the pinkness of it," he murmured. "Why is it pretending to be an elephant? Ridiculous! There aren't any pink elephants in the Kingdom of the Sharpeyes." He sniffed deeply. "Aha, I can smell something! It's very faint, but I'm sure there's a hint of Blah-blah scent here," he declared. "And where have I seen round spinners like this before?" he wondered.

"The sandstorm!" exclaimed Little Dream. "We heard that *vroom-vroom* noise!"

"So we did, by all that's juicy!" cried Uncle. "So that *was* the sound we heard on the night of the storm! The Blah-blahs must have been using a Vroom-vroom to get away from the storm!" He had a thought. "Wait! Keep sharp!" Suddenly he was racing up to the top of the ridge again.

He moved along it, bobbing up and down, twisting his neck to point his one eye, always on the look-out. He could see Black Thorn Hill where some of the tribe were going about their business. Some were still foraging and others were taking a nap in the shade. But Uncle had something else on his mind.

"I've found tracks!" he called down to the kits, "…and here! Tracks, side by side! You're right, Little Dream! A Vroom-vroom certainly did come along this way. But why here? They usually stay

83

over by the Salt Pans on the far side of the kingdom. There have never been any of them this close to the birth-burrow!"

"Perhaps it got lost in the storm – because of all the flying sand and stones," suggested Skeema.

"Good thinking, my clever young kit!" exclaimed Uncle and scrambled down the slope again. "Let me take a closer look at this thing. Mind out, Little Dream. That's a royal command by the way!" He gave him a wink. He hadn't felt so lively and excited for ages.

Mimi had found a ring sticking out from one end of the shell. She tugged at it playfully. A long strap stretched out and then snapped back. She ran behind Uncle for protection.

"How big are Vroom-vrooms?" asked Skeema, wondering if this was one.

"Oh, massive!" said Uncle. "Much bigger than this. The ones I saw, you could get a whole tribe of four or five Blah-blahs inside them."

"Well, maybe this shell is a special nursery chamber!" said Skeema. "Maybe the Vroom-vroom we heard was carrying it to a safe place. But then it dropped it by mistake and the storm covered it over with sand!"

"A nursery chamber… of course! Brilliant!" exclaimed Uncle.

"But there's no way in or out of it," Mimi said, peeping out from behind Uncle. "If you want to know what I think… I think it's an elephant's egg."

"Hmm. Let's give it a shake and see if we can hear anything," suggested Uncle. "Lend a paw, there! Shaky-shake-shake!" Something inside it went click, then…

CRACK!

Suddenly it split open right down the middle and its insides flew everywhere.

It was quite a while before Fearless dared to peek out from under the bush where he and the kits had dived for cover. He was relieved to see that nothing was moving on the sand dune. He felt the kits pushing impatiently behind him.

"Hurry up, Uncle!" said Mimi. "I'm starving! Let's go and see if the inside of an elephant's egg is worth eating."

"We're all hungry, Mimi," snapped Uncle, "but safety first! Keep together close behind me and don't touch anything until I give the order."

The insides of the elephant-shaped shell had scattered over quite a wide area. Very cautiously Uncle began to gather things up into a pile and inspect them. "Aha!" he announced. "Yes… I'm pretty sure all these things belong to a Blah-blah.

And as you say, Skeema, this very well *could* be a mobile nursery chamber. It has spinners, after all, and all these things probably belong to a very young Blah-blah. Now, let me see if I can recognise anything."

He made a little pile.

"These," he announced importantly, "are for a youngster to chew, I think. They're not food exactly. But I've definitely seen young Blah-blahs with these in their mouths. No doubt they sharpen their teeth on them. Now, what else can I tell you about?"

'Whatever is this?" asked Mimi. She held out a little box. Inside were a number of perfectly round smooth stones. They sparkled in the sunshine.

"Look!" she gasped. "You can see right through them. Look at the lovely coloured whirly lines twisting round inside them!"

Little Dream stared at the stones. "Like eyes," he said to himself.

"I've see these hanging on the darkness in the Upworld when the suntime is gone," said Uncle. "The Blah-blahs love to watch them. They call them stars."

"They must be for the baby to watch when it hatches," said Skeema.

"Put them in the backpack," said Uncle already turning to look at something else.

"Aha!" he exclaimed. He picked up a shiny, boxy thing. "Now this is an eye-protector, by all that crawls in damp sand! Didn't I tell you about seeing these before, in my Glory Days, when I was a young king, exploring my kingdom! Many's the time the Chief of the Click-clicks bowed down in front of me. He was too nervous to look at me without protecting his eyes – like this." Bold King Fearless put the shiny thing in front of his face.

"Oh, *please*!" muttered Skeema through gritted teeth. "He's not going to start on his Glory Days again, is he?"

Uncle put down what he was holding and picked up something else. "These are interesting. I've seen these before. I can't quite remember what they're for. Possibly weapons of some kind." He lifted one to his ear and shook it hard.

"Weapons? Like teeth and claws?" teased Mimi. "Well, I must say, they look *really* sharp… **not**!"

"Oh, well, you're probably right," said Uncle, with a shrug. Hup! He tossed it high into the air towards a pile of jagged rocks in a gulley below them.

It landed. There was a mighty… **BLATT!**

…and the thing let out a hiss louder than a whole nest of cobras. It spat a long jet of evil-looking brown liquid high in the air.

Before the last of it splattered among the rocks, the little gang had scattered and lay quaking under the bush again.

"What was *that?*" gasped Skeema, his heart pounding.

"Snake-in-a-canister," said Uncle grimly. "Deadly! You give the canister a rough shake, you pull the ring on the top and the snake inside squirts a deadly poison at your enemy. I've seen the Blah-blah males practising with these weapons sometimes at sun-down."

They spread out. Cautiously they sniffed out the other scattered contents of the shell. Nothing was moving, so they became bolder. Soon they had made another little pile.

"Hmmm! Well, now, Mimi, this (sniff-sniff) is definitely Blah-blah food," declared Uncle.

"About time!" said Mimi.

"Yum yum," said Little Dream, licking his lips.

"Can we eat now?" said Skeema. "I'm shrinking."

"Very well, but no fighting!" warned Uncle. "We'll share the food. Mimi, you can have this little snake with the funny nose. Little Dream can have the yellow blind-lizard. Skeema and I will share this nest of grubs."

They tucked in hungrily. Mimi didn't think much of her snake. It made her mouth go all frothy. Little Dream quite enjoyed his lizard, once he had bitten its head off. It was better than giant millipedes, anyway.

In spite of what Uncle had said, Skeema started a little fight to get the nest of grubs for himself. He and Uncle had a growly tug-of-war for a moment. Then the nest suddenly burst with a loud ripping sound and a shower of red and pink and blue and green and orange grubs flew everywhere. Uncle had to be quick to grab some for himself. And what a disappointment! How horribly sweet and gummy they were! How they stuck to their back teeth!

"If this is the sort of food that Blah-blahs eat, they can keep it! Yuck!" said Skeema, spitting it out. The taste reminded him of some powdery stuff he once licked off a bee's legs. He considered stealing some of Little Dream's lizard but changed his mind when Little Dream was sick on the spot.

Chapter 9

Skeema thought he had seen something jump quite a long way out of the chamber when it split open. It wasn't long before he sniffed it out. It was trying to hide under a rock but the lime-green tail sticking out gave it away. Skeema sank his teeth into it. The creature squeaked loudly, but Skeema held on bravely and dragged it into the bright sunlight. The creature didn't move, so he got it in a death-grip and squeezed. *Squeak! Squeak!* it cried.

"That's odd," thought Skeema. "It should be dead." He nipped it all over. *Squeak! Squeak! SQUEAK!*

Uncle came over to help. "Be careful," he warned. "I have heard tales of these creatures. They live under the big water in the land of the Narrowhead meerkats. They grow into enormous monsters and their jaws go snap-snap! Have you finished him off?"

"This is amazing!" said Skeema. "He ought to be dead but he just won't give up. Watch."

He bit the creature.

It squeaked.

"I like him! He's tough! And he smells nice. I'm going to keep him as my pet," Skeema announced.

Uncle was just about to advise Skeema against this when he heard a terrified cry.

"Help!" cried Mimi. "Little Dream's climbed into the pink chamber. He says there's an enemy meerkat hiding there! I think he's having a fight!"

"It could be a Ruddertail, by all that sneaks and slides!" roared Uncle Fearless. "Take cover, you two, and don't come out of your hiding place till I give the command." He let out a blood-chilling war cry and charged towards the open shell. "Hold on, Little Dream! I'll save you!"

With one bound he leaped over the side, ready to do or die. "Have at you!" he cried, swashing away with his digging claws. And then he exclaimed, "Woa, up!" He suddenly realised that

Little Dream didn't need his support. The smallest of all the Sharpeyes was locked in a life-and-death-struggle, all right.

Uncle breathed a sigh of relief. He had seen the sort of thing that Little Dream was fighting before and he racked his brain to remember what they were called. He remembered how small Blah-blahs wandering among their pointy mounds liked to carry around little models of themselves and stroke them and wave them. And when they dropped them, they would pick them up and hold them tight and call their names softly. Now what was it they called out? *"There-there!"* That was it! Little Dream had picked a fight with a There-there!

"Enemy meerkat!" panted Little Dream. "He tried to kill the Blah-blah egg." Growling fiercely, he sank his little teeth into 'the enemy' again and gave him a good shake. "But he can't hurt him now!"

"Well, er, look here, jolly good show, what-what!" said Uncle. It seemed a pity to mention that There-theres were harmless. As for the 'enemy meerkat' Little Dream had fought so fiercely, it was nothing more than a reflection of himself in the There-there's dark, flat eyes. Little Dream had clearly not understood when he told him before what Blah-blah eyes looked like. Besides, Uncle remembered exactly how frightened *he* had felt when he first saw himself mirrored in the eyes of the Chief of the Click-clicks.

"Brave work, you young spitter!" said Uncle. "You've conquered your first enemy all right! You won't have any more trouble from him! Here, try his eyes on. You've earned them." He slipped them on to the proud little kit's nose and put the arms behind his ears. "Nobody will tease you about pale eye-patches now, what-what! Here, put this on too." He also slipped the strap of the eye-protector round his neck. "There! Now you look like the Chief of the Click-clicks!" he laughed.

Little Dream was amazed. "Hooray! I can see much better!" he cried and jumped up and down for joy. "I can look up at the bright sky now, look!"

Uncle interrupted. "Listen, where's this egg that you say the enemy meerkat was after?"

Little Dream pointed to something that was strapped to the other half of the chamber. It *did* seem to be some sort of egg! It was at least twice meerkat-size, in a shiny gold shell and tied with sparkling ribbon.

Uncle scratched his head. "Well, well!" he exclaimed. "So that's what Blah-blah eggs look like!"

With a *Wee-ooo-ooo-ooo!* he sounded the all-clear for Skeema and Mimi and then quickly undressed the There-there. It looked very strange without any covering. Its body was brown and furless, and felt as hard and smooth as the walls of the pink chamber in which it travelled. It was nothing like the warm, soft, giant Blah-blah he had tamed and climbed up all that time ago. It made Uncle feel uncomfortable. He felt peculiar. There was something here he couldn't understand at all. So he solved the problem the meerkat way… by quickly burying it and forgetting about it.

He looked down at the pile of the There-there's clothes, and picked up the pith helmet. He tried it on. "Hmm, fits me rather well," he said to himself. "Good. I'll take these too." He put on the safari scarf and the backpack and felt very dashing. "I dare say I look rather splendid!" he told himself. "Rather like a Blah-blah Chief, I imagine!"

Skeema was first to reappear, closely followed by Mimi. Little Dream was naturally very keen to show off his new eyes. He was expecting his brother and sister to be surprised, but he wasn't ready for what happened when they saw him. Their happy expressions changed to looks of alarm. They let out their wildest attack-calls. They puffed themselves out and started doing what they hoped was a fearsome war dance!

"Stand easy!" ordered Uncle, chuckling. "Relax! There's no danger! Use your noses! It's only your little brother. Can't you smell him?!"

Skeema and Mimi could *smell* that it was only Little Dream, but their eyes told them that he looked suddenly stronger, sharper and... well, scarier.

"What happened?" they wanted to know.

"Oh, let's just say that he was faced with a difficult test – and he did very well," said Uncle. "And I for one am very proud of him."

"Us too!" said Skeema and Mimi. They gave him a squeeze and congratulated him. Little Dream went all shy and modestly lifted his new eye-protector in front of his face. "No, honestly! That was really brave, Dreamie. Well done," they said, and meant it.

Uncle picked up the There-there's little desert boots. "Here, these are for you, Skeema," he said. "Wear these on your back paws. They'll keep your claws nice and sharp and shiny, ready for action."

"Squeak!" said the lime-green Snap-snap

tucked under Skeema's arm, as if he thought they looked pretty cool too.

"Mimi now, me! Me!" said Mimi.

"I have just the thing for you, my dear," said Uncle. "This piece of soft nesting material is very pretty and it will alarm your enemies. Here, wrap it around yourself."

Mimi was delighted. "Am I like a female Blah-blah?" she said to Uncle, her wide eyes shining.

"Most certainly!" said Uncle kindly. "If they have princesses among the Blah-blahs, I'm sure they look like you."

The talk of princesses made Little Dream think about their mother, Fragrant, who was taken from them before he could remember. Still, at least he and his brother and sister had Uncle Fearless to take care of them.

He put his arms around the egg. "Poor egg!" he said quietly. "What will he do without his mamma? The Vroom-vroom's gone without him!"

"Far away to the other side of the kingdom, I'm afraid," sighed Uncle.

Little Dream held his ear close to the egg. "I can hear his heart," he said.

"Let Mimi listen! Me! Me!" demanded Mimi and pressed her ear against the shiny shell too. When they listened carefully, they could all hear the egg's heart beating. *Bic-tic-bic-tic*.

"Quick!" said Uncle. "I think we should close the chamber. We mustn't let the egg get cold." He gathered up the things that were lying about. He put all the shiny canisters into his backpack, bundled the rest of the stuff into the pink chamber next to the egg and closed it with a snap. No sooner had he stood it up on its spinners than his ears pricked up and his eye began to dart about. He thought he heard a whispering sound from underground. Or was it the sound of loose stones tumbling down a sand dune?

"We're coming to *get* you!" came a sing-song voice; a high, pretending-to-be-a-kit voice. Then there was sniggering. It sounded hollow, out of tune. It was coming from out of a bolthole that wasn't far away! "Now, what kind of far-fetched stories has that naughty old chatterbox been telling them, I wonder?" it teased.

Chapter 10

Uncle Fearless bristled and dragged the kits close to him. They could feel his growling and spit-calls vibrating through his tense body as he stood on all four paws, more like a lion than a meerkat. "I smell strangers," he whispered and then he raised his voice into a challenge. "Show yourselves if you want a fight!"

The sniggers turned to laughter. Were there three voices? "Don't worry, old timer! There's not really going to be a fight... yet!"

"Who are you? Narrowheads? Then what are

doing so far from your own territory? Come out of your hole and face me," challenged Fearless.

"Face *us*, he means!" said Skeema, showing his teeth. "There are four fighters here!"

"Hi-yip-yip!" Mimi and Little Dream joined in. "Come on! We're not scared of you!"

Suddenly, there was a scrabbling noise and a large, grey Narrowhead male sprang up between them and the safety of the burrow entrance. At the same moment, an even larger brute leapt out from a hole hidden under a tussock of buffalo grass. There was no mistaking his misshapen silvery head or the twisted diggers on his right paw.

"Twisted Claw!" breathed Uncle.

"Hello, Fearless! So, they've left you to mind the babies and the burrow, have they? Is that all you're fit for these days – babysitting? Dear, oh dear! Not much to brag about, is it? You used to think you were so high and mighty! Always going on about how the Blah-blahs let you climb all over them and tame them. And as for them bringing you eggs and nuts to eat! Well, we've heard a rumour that you offered *yourself* as a meal for an eagle owl! Is that right? Did you *really* stand about in the open Upworld like some sleepy little grasshopper who hasn't got a clue about keeping a proper look-out? No wonder you've only got one eye and you're a nobody! Fearless may be your name, but it's not your nature, is it? You're nothing but an old windbag!"

Twisted Claw's bodyguard threw back his ugly head and laughed like a hyena.

For a moment the strength drained out of Uncle. He glanced at the kits and felt ashamed. What must they think of him now? The kits said nothing but were bracing themselves for an attack. They sensed, as Uncle surely did, that the

Narrowheads were softening them up.

Suddenly Twisted Claw made a quick and secret series of whistling calls. In the flick of an eyelid, the bodyguard stopped laughing and began ducking and weaving like a snake getting ready to strike.

Faced with a half-blind old wreck of a Sharpeye and a bunch of mewling kits, Twisted Claw and his bodyguard would normally have walked right over them. Yet for all their outward swagger, they felt far from sure of themselves. For a start, there was something peculiar about Fearless's appearance that made them hesitate. What was that strange object on his battered head? That thick collar? The floating material round his shoulders? What was the curious thing that he had strapped to his back like another belly?

And it wasn't only the oddness of *his* appearance that rattled them. The kits looked a bit… well, *mad* too! The female had something bright and flapping wrapped round her body. One of the young males was holding out some sort of dangerous-looking reptile in a very threatening manner. And as for the little one – what enormous scary eyes he had! Dark and square!

They only hesitated for a second, but it was enough time for Uncle to recover his wits. "Ask yourself something, Twisted Claw," he said calmly. "If I never tamed any Blah-blahs, or made them my subjects, why did they give me all this to protect my body?" He stretched out his arms to present himself in his Safari-Man outfit.

"And do you see this chamber?" He drummed it sharply with his claws. "This is a Blah-blah egg chamber. I am in charge of it."

"Yes, and we're going to take it to the Blah-blah mounds on the far side of the kingdom!" Little Dream suddenly blurted out.

"We're going on an adventure. We're going to take it back to its mamma!"

Of course, Uncle wasn't expecting this. All he could do when he heard what Little Dream said was gulp and nod his head in agreement. "Er… yes. He's quite right, Twisted Claw! You're interrupting a very important… um, m-mission!" he stammered.

With that the tables suddenly turned again. Twisted Claw puffed up his fur and became bolder. His voice sounded foxy. "A mission, you say? There's no need for that. Why don't we save you the trouble? Give us the chamber. We've always wanted to try taming Blah-blahs ourselves, haven't we, Patchie?"

His bodyguard nodded. "Too true!" he rumbled. "And what could be better to attract their attention than something as big and bright as this, eh?" He began to speak fast and urgently to

Twisted Claw. "I reckon we should just grab it quick, Chief, because the rest of the Sharpeye mob might turn up here any minute! You flatten this mad old windbag and leave the kitties to me. They won't give us too much trouble. They're only like a bunch of little scorpions doing a crazy dance to try to put us off, that's all."

Mimi snatched one of the shiny canisters from Uncle's backpack. "Don't you dare call me a crazy scorpion. And do not touch me, not Mimi! Not me," she shouted in a shrill voice. "I've got a deadly weapon!" She shook the canister wildly.

"So have I!!" cried Skeema, holding up his Snap-snap and squeezing it. Its piercing SQUEAK! shocked the Narrowheads and they jumped back a pace.

As it happened, there was no need for either Mimi or Skeema to test their weapons in battle. Suddenly there was a noise like the snapping of a

twig and a blinding bolt of lightning shot out of
Little Dream's chest!

Two more dazzling flashes followed in quick
order, and before the last of them faded, the
terrified Narrowheads had upped tails and run for
their lives.

"Whoops!" said Little Dream. "All I did was
touch this little lump here…" There was another

deadly flash that had his brother and sister and his Uncle squealing and diving for cover. "Sorry," said Little Dream, just before he fell flat on his back. "Is everybody all right?"

Chapter 11

After the group had recovered from the shock of
Little Dream's daring surprise attack, they sat
excitedly going over what had just happened.

"My goodness, Little Dream !" Uncle exclaimed
with a gasp. "Whatever made you come up with
that nonsense about us taking the egg chamber to
the Blah-blah mounds? I nearly had a fit,
what-what!"

"Sorry, Uncle," said Little Dream. "I just
wanted you to be proud of me."

Uncle was touched. "I am, dear boy, I'm very

proud of you. But as for striking out across the desert on our own, that's quite ridic—"

"I should like to go to Far Burrow!" interrupted Mimi. She had made up her mind. "Uncle, why *don't* we return the egg to its mother and then go and live by the Salt Pans for ever and ever? I don't want to stay here with our horrid Queen Heartless."

"Me neither! I should love to see those Blah-blah mounds," agreed Skeema. "Let's all run away and go there *now!* Go on, Uncle," he pleaded. "Take us to Far Burrow. You wouldn't have to be a babysitter any more. You could be a proper king again!"

"Me? A king again? You can't really suppose that… I mean to say… Come on! It's not that I've forgotten how to *be* one or anything, what-what! It's quite true that I can dish out orders and terrify the enemy as well as the next royal meerkat…"

"And you can have lots more bold adventures

among the Blah-blah tribes!" squealed Little Dream. "We all can. We like adventures!"

"Well, my kits," laughed Uncle. "It's tempting, I must say. I'm getting ancient and rusty but you're all getting pretty bold and quick and tricky. Still, you don't know what you're asking for. You've just seen how nasty Narrowheads can be. Wait till you see the Ruddertails!"

"We're not scared of Ruddertails!" cried Skeema.

Uncle smiled and ruffled the fur on his head. "It must be true what everybody keeps saying. Just listen to us! We must all have The Madness even to *think* about making such a long journey. And there are going to be all sorts of dangers every step of the way. "

"And I don't like it here," said Mimi firmly. "I want to be in a story about how important I am."

Uncle took in a huge breath. "Right! That's settled then. We'll have no more negative nonsense! It's time to be positive. It's time to ACT! We four mad meerkats WILL travel to see the Blah-Blah mounds and we SHALL live to tell a tale or two, by all that's strong and tasty!" And to show he meant business, he lifted his tummy-pad with both paws. HUP! "And how are we going to do it?" he went on. "Altogether now!" He raised his paws above his head like a conductor.

The kits bunched together, lifted their chins high and with one voice, they proudly spoke the words of their motto:

"Stay alert to stay alive!

And stay with the group!"

For a giggle they pretended they were as fat as Uncle. They stuck out their tummies and lifted them up with both paws, shouting – 1-2-3-HUP!

Then they got going.

Chapter 12

Fear helped the madcap travellers on the first part of the journey. They ran as fast as they possibly could with a heavy egg chamber to drag along with them. Every now and then they thought they could hear scampering claws and they would turn expecting to see the Narrowheads or perhaps some angry Sharpeyes chasing after them, but it was only the wind or the rattling of pebbles behind them. They saw neither stripe nor tail of any other meerkat.

Once they had left the dunes behind, the
ground grew hard and sloped gently down towards
The Great Plain. The going was rough and bumpy,
but at least the chamber didn't keep sinking into
soft sand. In fact, now and again, the chamber
seemed to have the power to run forward by itself

like the crazy pink elephant it pretended to be.

When they reached The Great Plain, the way grew softer again. The kits were tired and began to struggle. Uncle was very jumpy. He knew that they must push on to safer ground before they could forage for food and find somewhere to sleep for the night. There was too little cover here for his liking, and too many chances to be trodden flat by the blundering monsters of the Upworld – the rhinos, the herds of antelope and zebras, the trumpeting elephants. The kits found it hard to believe that the lions, lying about in yawning dusty-yellow heaps, were not interested in meerkat snacks. Still, nothing scared them more than snakes. The quick, black ones were the worst. And the later it got, the more every whisper of the grasses began to sound like the hiss of a lurking mamba or puff adder.

As for Uncle, the thought of attack from out of the sun made all his once-broken bones ache. He imagined that everywhere in the sky, powerful birds of prey wheeled and mocked and screamed. His bent arm throbbed and there was a pain all down his side where his ribs had been shattered when he had dropped from a great height. At least he had his helmet and his pack. They gave *some* sort of protection.

As they travelled, Uncle sang lively contact songs, expecting the kits to echo the words to show that they were still there, that they were safe.

> "Look about, look about!
> (*Look about, look about*)!
> Listen out, listen out!
> (*Don't shout! Listen out!*)
> Don't know the sound?
> (*New sound! Wrong sound!*)
> Get underground!
> (*Dive underground!*)"

Uncle was right to be cautious. High in the cloudless blue, out of sight even from the keen eyes of young Skeema and Mimi, The Silent Enemy was watching.

The eagle-owl had only one thought in his revolving head: *revenge*.

The hot air lifted the eagle owl like waves holding up a swimmer in a warm sea. He kept his back to the sun and was careful not to show himself as more than a scratch in the sky. His sight was so powerful that when the meerkats were on open ground he could clearly see the sun glinting in the one busy eye that was still in Fearless's head. Each time it flashed, the eagle owl felt a twinge along his breastbone where Fearless's needle-sharp teeth had sunk in and made him scream and let go.

He knew that there is no more watchful a creature than a meerkat. But he was patient. There would be a moment when Fearless was off guard. One careless moment was all it would take, when his mind was on something else.

"Then," thought the eagle owl, "I shall drop like the darkness and dine on him! Oooo-hooo-hooo!"

When at last the worn-out travellers came to a place where devil's claw bushes, bright with yellow flowers, grew everywhere, Uncle breathed a sigh of relief. "Ground-squirrel territory!" he said. And sure enough, dozens of them popped up like little jack-in-the-boxes, flicking their charming bushy tails over their heads or swishing them out behind them. They nibbled at the yellow flowers and chattered among themselves.

"Can you speak their language?" Skeema asked Uncle.

"I'm afraid not," said Uncle. "But they are welcoming creatures. And we have an ancient agreement with all their tribes: we always give them shelter if they need it and they give shelter to us."

The travellers stopped and refreshed themselves, taking it in turns to dig for juicy roots to quench their thirst.

"Ouch!" squealed Little Dream, pricking himself on a wickedly sharp thorn for the umpteenth time. He was hungry, though, and he soon found plenty of strange-looking crawlers to fill his belly and make him forget the soreness of his nose.

And sure enough, as their shadows began to stretch, a motherly-looking ground squirrel with a broad stripe down her side led the way for them into a cool and pleasant-smelling burrow full of tumbling babies!

Chapter 13

A good sleep in the freezing darktime, snug among the soft bodies of the ground squirrel family, did the travellers good.

After a good Warm-up and a breakfast, they thanked their hosts and waved goodbye. They struggled on, often wishing that they could leave the egg chamber behind, because it took such an effort to keep it moving. They didn't stop for rest until they came to a red ebony tree that Uncle knew well. It spread its branches widely and offered them its cool shade for rest and shelter from the sun which was now at its hottest. Overhead the weaver birds flitted in and out of the holes in their enormous nest, chit-chatting busily.

"Is that what the Blah-blah mounds look like?" Mimi enquired. "I can't really picture them."

"Not quite. It's hard to explain exactly how they look. But with luck, we'll see them soon enough," said Uncle. He told them a little yarn to try and make things clearer, but he got a bit muddled and the tale fizzled out.

Skeema felt rather sorry for him. "You know, it doesn't really matter if there's no such thing as a Blah-blah, Uncle," he said kindly. "Whatever happens, we're all together now, and that's what's important. And it's a jolly good story, in any case!"

For once, Uncle was completely lost for words.

"I love it," murmured Little Dream sleepily.

Then the kits tumbled and fought for a short while until they fell over, fast asleep in a heap.

When they heard the thunder of springbok and gemsbok hooves, they twitched and jumped up again, heads turning all around.

"They won't hurt you," murmured Uncle, half-asleep. But his ears pricked up when he heard the shout of jackals and the cackle of hyenas. Suddenly all his brave little daredevils were burrowing under him like chicks under a mother weaver bird! "Far away," he said soothingly. "Safe here."

Above them The Silent Enemy cursed. He had no trouble seeing the pink, lumbering thing that the meerkats were dragging along, but the grasses kept hiding Fearless's eye, the one particular morsel he longed to taste more than any other. And now that the meerkats were under a tree, he could see nothing at all of the adult or the kits.

Once they had their strength back, the adventurers moved on and soon found themselves among golden grasses that whispered in the hot wind.

The spinners of the heavy chamber were useless in soft sand. The meerkats heaved but couldn't get it to go in a straight line. It had to be pulled along a twisting path in and out among the tall tufts. For an age no one said a word, except to answer Uncle's call. No one complained about their sore paws, not even Skeema who found that his little desert boots rubbed – but wouldn't take them off for all the ants' eggs in Africa. Little Dream did his best to keep pace with the others, though it was hard for him. Sometimes they let him ride on

130

top of the chamber and be look-out for a while to keep his spirits up.

"You remind me of a Blah-blah female I once saw riding on a camel," said Uncle with a wink at Skeema and Mimi. "She went wibble-wobble, wibble-wobble, *squeak!*"

"Why did she go wibble-wobble squeak, Uncle?" asked Little Dream. "Was she scared?"

"Ah!" said Uncle mysteriously, putting a claw

down the side of his nose to show he was telling a secret. "She didn't squeak while she was *on* the camel," said Uncle. "Only when she got off."

"But that's silly. If she wasn't wibble-wobbling any more, what did she squeak for?" Mimi wanted to know.

"I think it was because the camel spat in her eye!" said Uncle. And he laughed so much at his terrible joke that his big tummy went wibble-wobble and set the kits cackling with laughter like red-billed oxpeckers.

A bit of fun made a tough journey a little easier. Even so, it seemed an age before, at last, Uncle said the words the kits were waiting to hear: "Not far now before we rest." He was pointing with his long rust-tipped tail. "You see that red dune in the distance? There's a fine burrow there where we can shelter for the darktime."

But oh, what a painful 'little way' that was. By the time they had dragged themselves and their heavy load to the entrance to Red Dune Burrow, they felt half-dead.

The egg chamber had to be safely buried before they could finally crawl through the main entrance and into a cool, damp, safe place. "Well done!" said Uncle, at last. "In we go then." But something made him nervous. "Wait! Stand back!" He lifted his long nose and snuffed the air.

"A cobra, by all that spits," he said softly. "Can you hear that sound like the whispering grass? He's uncoiling, what-what! That's the sound of dry scales rubbing together!"

Chapter 14

The cobra was not pleased to be disturbed.

"SSSSteer clear!" he hissed. "I'm the lord of this burrow."

"You, sir, are no such thing. You are a squatter!" shouted Uncle indignantly. "I helped to build this burrow myself long ago. Now I should like to rest and shelter here and so would these kits. Kindly slither off and find another hole."

"Mind your manners or I'll *have* you!" warned the snake. He put his head out of the burrow and looked at them with killer eyes like small, licked stones. His head and hood were shiny black, though when he spread out the hood to scare them, the kits saw that it was marked with angry red blotches. Uncle had seen cheeks swollen with poison like this before. The brute was, as Uncle's nose had told him, a zebra spitting cobra. Underground, his grey belly would be striped with glittering bands. Because he wanted to keep the burrow for himself, he was not keen to show this part of himself just yet.

"Scorpion dance," said Uncle quietly to the kits, out of the corner of his mouth. "He can't hear much but he can lip-read. Now pay attention." He turned his head slightly, without taking his good eye off the intruder in case of attack. "Stay on your toes and remember the steps. He'll be quick, so you dance quicker!

Remember the snake-in-the-canister? That's how he'll go for you. He'll spit – and he can spit a long way. But if he spits, then mind your eyes! Skeema – here's the plan…"

The snake began to hiss like a burning branch in a wild fire. Though he was very deaf, he sensed that the meerkats were plotting something. His tongue flicked out, hoping to scent their fear. His jaws opened like a trap and when Skeema danced towards him, showing his teeth, he flicked his head in his direction. Skeema skipped away – and out of sight.

The cobra was well-pleased. Terror was a fine weapon. As the little female darted towards him, he pulled back again and this time sprayed twin jets of venom through his hollow fangs. The venom flew three metres but Mimi gave a squeal and, spinning like a little furry ballerina, she pirouetted out of danger.

"Good work, Mimi! Ten out of ten for style!"
cheered Uncle.

The hood was spreading again, the cheeks were
swelling, and the snake was forced to slither
forward. He tried to lift himself up in the confined
space of the burrow and wipe the look of triumph
off Uncle's face.

137

"Yikessssssss!" he fizzed. " What the…?"

"Has something just struck you?" enquired Uncle Fearless, innocently. He knew very well what it was that had just struck the cobra… and where. The sharp teeth of young Skeema had just locked on to his pointed backside! Uncle had sent the nipper down and round through a side-entrance to do just that.

The cobra had no room to turn back on himself, so he darted forward, his curved fangs reaching for Uncle's helmeted head. But Uncle knew the dance and stepped aside, his safari scarf swinging like a mini-matador's cape.

"Dance with *me*! With *me, again*!" cried Mimi. Furiously, the snake lunged at her. Half of him was out of the burrow now. They could see his zebra belly stripes clearly.

Meanwhile, Skeema was hanging on to his tail like grim death.

"Yoo-hoo!" squeaked Little Dream. When the cobra saw a rival snake reflected in Little Dream's eye-patches, he got so angry that his jaws almost came unhinged. He leapt clear of the burrow and would have punctured the brave little kit had Uncle not taken a running jump and pushed Little Dream out of the way.

Skeema was whipped into the air by the pointed tail his teeth were locked on to. He came down on the back of the cobra's neck like a cowboy on a bucking bronco. Holding on to the hood with one paw, he gave his Snap-snap a mighty *SQUEAK!* with the other as he landed. He then pushed both sides of the hood down over the eyes of his mount, gave him one more nip on the back of the neck for luck – and then jumped sideways to the ground.

This was all too much for the intruder. With one last hiss, he gathered his coils and shot off into the falling darkness.

Chapter 15

One dry river bed usually leads to another. For a long while there seemed no end to the dull and dusty yellow ways before them.

But at last they came to a greyish track that stretched out across the rolling sand hills. They scrambled up out of the river bed and followed this smoother way to the brow of a hill, delighted to find that the egg chamber ran very nicely along it on its spinners. They had expected a long, slow haul and were surprised to make good, quick progress.

"Not much further now!" said Uncle cheerily. "This flat track was made by the Blah-blahs. See how wide it is, and how straight? And it has been trodden down so that they can move their Vroom-vrooms along it. Sometimes these tracks have no end, but often they lead directly to the mounds of one Blah-blah tribe or another. So stay extra sharp, what-what!" He patted Little Dream on the head. "And just keep it in mind that Vroom-vrooms can run faster than cheetahs. We must be careful. Why, I remember one time, in my Glory Days, I was wandering…"

At that moment, his words were cut off by a dreadful roar. All heads turned towards the sound and all eyes saw a cloud of dust leap just over the rise. "Take cover! Run for your lives!" yelled Uncle.

In the panic, everyone jerked the egg chamber in different directions. It tottered and crashed sideways.

"Get it over the side! Get it over the side!" yelled Uncle. "It'll be crushed!"

The kits had to overcome their instinct to dive off the road and disappear into the bush that grew thickly on either side of it. But having come this far as a team, they were all determined to be ruled by Uncle and not by blind fear.

"Hold on, Uncle! We're coming!" they cried and gathered alongside him to put their backs into the task. But pushing an egg chamber lying on its side was very much harder than pulling it upright on its spinners.

"It won't budge!" panted Skeema.

"It feels dreadfully heavy!" puffed Mimi. She dashed round to the other side and found that a long flat stone had wedged underneath it. She got her claws under it and tried to scratch it away, but it was almost as big as she was. "There's a rock! It won't shift!" she shouted. Skeema left his post and darted round to help her. Their combined efforts did the trick and they moved the stone enough for Uncle and Little Dream to feel the chamber jerk forward when they put their shoulders to it.

"It's moving! It's starting to slide!" piped up Little Dream. The roaring was getting frighteningly close, as if a herd of Kalahari lions were leaping towards them.

At last the egg chamber began to shift, centimetre by centimetre, towards the edge. Mimi and Skeema managed to grab the strap and pull with all their might while the others continued to push. Suddenly it picked up speed and plunged to the side of the road. It reached a tipping point, wobbled – until finally it was flipped by its own weight over the edge.

Mimi and Skeema had to be quick to fling themselves out of its way into a bush, and the chamber itself crashed down and came to rest under a blue pea shrub.

Uncle had made a huge effort to save the chamber. Perhaps that was why, when it shot away from him, he fell hard on to his round belly and lay winded, unable to get up.

"Up!" said Little Dream who had been pushing too. He tugged at Uncle's backpack. The roaring dust cloud was getting horribly close.

"No good. No puff left. Leave me. Save yourself!" panted Uncle.

Little Dream turned his head and saw his first Vroom-vroom. He just had time to consider that this was also probably the last Vroom-vroom he would ever see. It was coming at him, with its silver mouth gaping and its golden eyes lit up, as terrifying as a charging bull rhinoceros.

"Run!" ordered Uncle and closed his one eye tight. His mind was racing. *I've had my ups and downs*, he was thinking, *but all in all it's been a*

good life. The kits are bright little things. They'll
cope without me. And at least it'll all be over
quickly…

Still lying face down, he tried to roll himself
into as small a ball as possible and put his paws
over his ears.

All of a sudden, he felt teeth tugging at the fur
on the back of his neck and found himself being
dragged, not towards the edge of the track, but
towards the middle.

It flashed through his mind that he had been
grabbed by a jackal or a bat-eared fox and he

147

struggled, weak as he was, to shake himself free. Then he was astonished to hear a voice he knew very well (though it came through teeth firmly clamped together) calling, "I've got you, Uncle!"

Fearless opened his eye and turned his head just enough to be able to see that it was Little Dream who had hold of him!

"Stop, Dreamie! Let go of me!" he panted. The kit seemed to have found enormous strength. "Wrong way!" he tried to tell him. "Save yourself!"

His voice was lost in the thunder of the engine sound.

Then the Vroom-vroom ran over them both.

Chapter 16

Mimi and Skeema were too stunned to move. They lay under a bush, sobbing in each other's arms, long after the thunder of the Vroom-vroom had become an angry hum and faded into the distance.

"My Uncle! My Dreamie!" wailed Mimi. "What am I going to do without them?"

"What about me?" sniffed her brother. "They were mine, too, you know!"

"Go up see what's happened to them. I can't bear to look," said Mimi. A horrible picture of a dead porcupine she had seen further down the track flashed into her mind. It had been squashed flat to twice its normal size.

"Me? What makes you think that I want to see them… like that!" snapped Skeema. He grabbed her paw. "Come on. We've got to make sure, but let's go and look together."

The thorns of the thick bushes into which they'd thrown themselves were devilishly sharp. They had to be careful to pick their way out and into the open. They were both expecting to have to face the worst sight they could ever imagine. So it wasn't surprising that Skeema forgot for the moment part of the Sharpeye motto: *Stay alert to stay alive*. That was the last thing on his mind as he scrambled up to the top branch of a tree and forced himself to peep down at the road.

At once, relief flooded through him, sweeter than scorpion-juice. He saw by some miracle – large as life and completely unhurt – dear old

Uncle Fearless sitting up in the road while Little
Dream fanned him with his helmet!

As it happened, it was almost the last thing he
saw. From the cloudless sky above them, a wicked
shadow was swooping with no sound, no warning.
It dropped
more swiftly
than the cold
darktime that
blots out the sun.

It was
The Silent Enemy.

Luckily, Mimi had her wits about her. One
danger can hide another and her keen eyes had
spotted one. She let out an ear-splitting alarm
call and knocked Skeema off his look-out post.
They tumbled headlong through thick, spiky

branches to the ground.

They both screamed with terror and braced themselves. At any second, each expected to be snatched from under the bush and hoisted into the air by a wicked bunch of dagger-sharp talons.

Out on the open road there were other yells and shrieks. These were followed by the eagle owl's hoot of triumph. A terrible silence followed. Then came Little Dream's defiant, "Take that, you big bully!" The eagle owl made one more dreadful, gargling sound and suddenly, Mimi and Skeema could see him through the tangle of leaves and branches above them! They watched the great bird struggling to take off with a wild flapping of wings that shook feathers off him like rain.

He seemed to be choking and spinning clumsily around. They could see his yellow eyes

152

were wide with terror as he battled to lift himself into the air.

"Oh no!" thought Skeema and tried to cover his sister's eyes with his paw. "He's got somebody in his claws!"

For a few more seconds, the wicked bird zigzagged and staggered just above the ground until, with a great effort, it heaved itself into the sky and was gone.

Skeema and Mimi hugged one another and trembled, not knowing what to do.

"Wheeee!" came a loud voice from above. Almost immediately, there was a crash as something dived into the bush they were hiding under.

"Is it the eagle owl? Has he come back for us now?" shrieked Mimi.

Another crash, louder than the first, followed by a shout. "Missed us, what-what!"

Branches were bent and snapped, leaves were smacked and twigs cracked – but not by The Silent Enemy.

"By all that roars and hoots, those were two close calls!" yelled Uncle, brushing sand out of his fur and straightening his collar, safari scarf and pith helmet. "I was certain I was no better than roadkill when the Vroom-vroom came charging at us," he panted, "but Little Dream here had different ideas, what-what!"

"I could see the spinners on the Vroom-vroom," gasped Little Dream. "They were fixed on each side, throwing up dust and stones. Still, I could see a gap between them and I *just* managed to drag Uncle into it. The Vroom-vroom ran right over the top of us but the spinners missed us completely! But, oh gosh! Then we saw The Silent Enemy."

"Oh, and he thought he'd got me properly
this time – the coward! The sneak! The
snake-in-the sky!"

"We saw him grab you, Uncle," said Mimi.
"We thought we'd never see you again!"

"Well, unluckily for him, all he got was my
backpack!" said Uncle with a laugh. "Ha-ha!
That'll be a tasty treat for him, don't you think?"

"Thank goodness you're both *alive!*" gasped Skeema, giving his dear old Uncle a hug and a warm wet scent-mark on both cheeks. "We thought you were both…" He managed to grab his little brother and give him bit of a hug, too. A *cheek-mark would be a bit much*, he thought, but he gave him good squeeze and a warm and brotherly pat on the back.

"Well, here we are, nearly dead, but not quite," said Uncle, who was starting to feel better already. "And all thanks to Little Dream."

"But it was you who taught me to keep a sharp look-out!" Little Dream piped up.

"Yes, well, that's kind of you to say so. But you kept your head! There's the thing. And you saved us both, by all that's sharp and lively!"

"What did he do, exactly?" asked Mimi.

"Well, there we were," said Uncle in his storytelling voice. "Me and this plucky little squirmer, both flat out in the road, me on my tummy and Dreamie on his back. I couldn't see a blessed thing. The dust from the Vroom-vroom was terrible! So there I was, blinded and thrashing about like a helpless kitty. Not a chance of spotting The Silent Enemy, of course. So he obviously thought – *Good show! Meerkat on the menu. Dive, dive, dive!*"

"But Dreamie saw him!" Skeema could picture it now.

"Thanks to my Blah-blah eyes," said Little Dream, modestly. "They let me look right into the sun if I want to!"

"He spotted the blighter all right! And quick as a cricket, he got his paw in my backpack. He felt around for the little box – and before you knew it, he'd grabbed one of the shiny round stars belonging to the baby Blah-blah."

"Ah! Did you hurl it at him? Did you clonk him

157

on his horrid beaky head with it?" asked Mimi, thinking that's just what she would have liked to do. "Craftier than that!" cried Uncle. "He held it in the flat of his paw and made it flash in the sunlight. That idiotic bird couldn't believe his luck! He thought *at last* he had the chance to grab the good eye I got away with last time he attacked me! But Little Dream had laid the perfect trap for him and the rotter fell for it! You could say..." said Uncle, wiping tears of mirth from his eye as he laughed at his own joke, "...you could say he *swallowed the thing whole*, what-what! Ha-ha! Hee-hee! And let's hope he jolly well chokes on it!"

"Little Dream!" cried Mimi. "What a big, brave meerkat you are!" She grabbed him and danced him off his paws.

"Brilliant!" cried Skeema. "And I thought I was the cunning one in our family!"

158

"Brilliant is the word!" chuckled Uncle. "So that blasted bird won't be bothering us again in a hurry." He shivered with relief. "Gosh, what a shake-up!" He gave himself a good flapping twitch to clear his mind.

"Plenty of shake-ups! That's what we all need!" said Mimi, joining in, shaking herself until her fur stood out like a mad little duster.

"Hear! Hear!" said Skeema with a giggle before joining in like a wet puppy and shaking himself all over, too.

That night, having found a burrow to sleep in, Uncle insisted on a group grooming session before bedtime to get rid of the tics they'd picked up on the journey.

After that, feeling very proud of everyone, Uncle kept watch under the stars for a time, while the youngsters slept safely below.

Chapter 17

The hills that had been in the misty distance for much of the journey were solid and up close by next suntime. After the near-thing with the Vroom-vroom they decided not to risk keeping to the road. That meant a lot of hard work to keep the egg chamber rumbling forward. The grasses grew greener and more lush and the scrub was thicker now. Still, excited about getting close to their goal, the little mob pushed on in good spirits.

They hadn't gone far when Mimi pointed out something hanging from the highest branch of a tall tree. "Look! It's your backpack, Uncle!" she cried. "Let me get it down for you!"

Mimi darted up the tree, agile as a monkey. "It *is* your backpack, Uncle!" she called down. "The Silent Enemy must have been disappointed that he wasn't clutching *you* in his claws! Wow – what a view from here!" She gasped. "I can see right across the valley to where it gets all grey and as flat as flat again!"

"The Salt Pans," chuckled Uncle. "I thought as much!"

"And look! There!" came Mimi's call again. She pointed and her tail-flag started waving as if it had The Madness in it. "I can see something interesting. Some sort of pointy termite mounds, I think!"

The others left the egg chamber where it was and scrambled up to her swaying perch to join her. "You're right!" said Uncle. "Those mounds are *very* interesting. But you won't find many termites in them!"

Suddenly he was clutching at all the kits and pulling them to him. His chin wobbled. It took him a little moment to be able to speak, and then he said quietly, "I know you must think I'm a bit of an old phony. And I have to admit that I can lay it on a bit thick about my Glory Days. I wouldn't blame you at all if you had made up your minds that everything I said about the Blah-blahs was just stories. But listen. You're now looking at something you'll be able to tell your own kits about one day. Right now, we are looking at some real, live, actual... Blah-blahs!"

The kits were struck dumb with wonder. They watched in astonishment as groups of charming giant creatures ventured out and moved on their hind legs among their strange, flapping dwelling places. They could see they were gigantic, even from a distance, and naked-looking, not having any fur, but for all their strangeness, they behaved just like meerkats in lots of ways! They dashed about together in family groups, slipping in and out of their pointy mounds. Then suddenly they were chattering and jumping up and down in an excited mob, pointing and calling *Oolook-look!* at something in the sky.

"Aren't they *funny!* Aren't they *cute!!*" cried Little Dream.

"They must have spotted those pink ibises and woolly-necked storks flying by!" laughed Skeema. "Oh! Silly things! They must think they're dangerous! They've put up those flappy warnings to scare them off. And look at the way they hide their eyes behind their little shiny boxes!"

"So *sweet* with their big monkey faces!" cooed Mimi. "How I'd love to hug one and stand on its head! Are they from the Oolook tribe, Uncle?" asked Mimi.

"I can't tell you till we get closer," said Uncle, with a shrug. "I'm afraid they all look the same to me from here." Then he pointed a little to the left at a lovely sandy spot deep in the valley not far from a group of the tallest, greenest trees they had ever seen. Their sheltering branches spread like umbrellas and made shadows as cool and inviting as underground chambers.

"That is Shepherd Tree Clump," said Uncle, with a lump in his throat. "And under that beautiful white sand – do you see? That's Far Burrow. That's where we're heading. That's our new home."

They stood for a moment, eyes glistening, swaying in the branches, without a care in the Upworld.

Then Skeema stiffened. He'd seen something. "Oh, no! We're not the only ones heading for Far Burrow by the look of it!" he said in dismay.

He pointed out something moving stealthily down through the grass tufts on the orange dunes on the other side of the valley.

"Oh no! By all that's impudent!" exclaimed Uncle. "It can't be…! Not this side of the Salt Pans, surely!"

Chapter 18

"My eye's not good enough to be sure at this distance, dash it! And those creatures are well beyond scenting range," growled Uncle. "Mimi. How about you, my dear? Can you make out their markings? I hope to goodness I'm mistaken and they're no more our enemies than ground squirrels?"

"It's not easy to tell exactly what they are from here," said Mimi. "They keep low and then dash from tuft to tuft."

"Cunning," murmured Uncle. "Lined or striped?"

"I can see one," exclaimed Skeema. "There he

goes… and he's striped!"

"I've got him," said Mimi. "Look how orange they are. Aha! I get it! That's how they can stay hidden against the dunes."

"Check the tails," urged Uncle.

"There's nothing bushy about them," said Mimi. "They're skinny and upright, most of them, very long and with dark red at the tip, not black like ours."

"Then it's as I feared. Those blighters are Ruddertails, or I'm a legless skink."

"Look! There are three more over there, by that bush," said Little Dreamer making the branch quiver as he pointed.

"I'll bet they're heading for The Grove," muttered Uncle. He was thinking of the thick hedge of plants where herds of antelope came to feed in the dry season. Now they were covered in pink and white flowers.

"The Ruddertails think they can keep out of sight there and then move together in among the shepherd trees," he told the others. "That way they'll be close enough to the burrow to see whether it's already occupied. I expect they'll lie low in the boltholes in the darktime and then prepare a surprise attack just after Warm-up. They'll note how many of the rightful owners come out to forage. Then once they're confident that they have the greater number – Vrrrrr! – they'll pounce!"

"An ambush, eh? So what's your plan, Uncle?" asked Skeema.

"Well, in my day the usual tactic was to bring up the whole tribe to dance in front of the burrow – show the enemy our teeth and claws, what-what! But…"

"But what, Uncle?" asked Mimi. She liked the idea of a face-to-face scrap.

"The trouble is, we won't have a lot of teeth and claws to show the blighters. There could easily be ten times more of them," said Uncle with a sigh. "We wouldn't stand a worm's chance!"

Skeema turned to look at his brother and saw himself reflected in his shiny new eyes. He liked what he saw and puffed out his fur. "I've got an idea," he said. "If the Ruddertails are planning to give us a little surprise, then maybe we should…"

Little Dream finished his sentence for him: "…give them an even bigger surprise!" he cried.

Chapter 19

The plan the group came up with meant that they had to move quickly. Before anything useful could be done to defend it, they must quickly claim the burrow and scent-mark the territory around it before the enemy arrived.

Dragging the egg chamber through the thick scrub was painful. There were roots and scratchy branches everywhere. Panting like wild dogs, the adventurers arrived at last at the lip of the steep valley and looked down towards the leafy greenness below.

They could clearly see the low sandy mounds that marked the entrances and escape tunnels. The problem now was that there was no cover. Hardly anything grew on the dry stony slope that led down to Far Burrow and its splendid foraging grounds.

"Even a mole-snake would be able to spot us if we started pulling a baby pink elephant down there!" groaned Skeema. "We wouldn't have a hope of surprising the enemy."

"You're right. We'll have to bury the egg-chamber here and collect it after the battle," said Uncle. They opened it to check the egg was safe. Mimi pressed her ear against it, making its shiny covering rustle. "I can still hear its heart beating," she said. "But it's very faint." *Bic-tic-bic-tic!* it went. She gave it a squeeze to warm it a bit.

The egg made a whirring sound and suddenly cried out in a strange sing-song voice:

"Happy birthday to you

Happy birthday to you!
Happy birthday, dear Charlie,
Happy birthday to you!"

Mimi was so shocked, she fell flat on her back. The others dived for cover. When the egg made no sign of speaking again, they crept back.

"What do you think, Uncle?" asked Little Dream.

"I think it must be about to hatch into a Blah-blah," said Uncle. "How strange! I had no idea that they could talk while they're still in their shells! But we haven't time to wait. We have a battle to fight and we must get into position, what-what! We'll just have to cover the egg to keep it warm and come back for it as soon as we can."

Quickly, he checked the weapons in his backpack. "Mimi, you'll take these snake-in-the-boxes. Skeema, see what you can do with these." He rattled the star-stones in their little box. Then he noticed something lying in the open egg chamber. "I'll take this black stick and sharpen my teeth on it," he said, and put it into his mouth while he and the others snapped the egg chamber shut and covered it in leaves and branches.

CLICK!

"Nga-nga," said Uncle, meaning to say, "*Well done*," but forgetting he had his mouth full. Suddenly, a blinding light shot out from the end of the stick. The kits squealed and covered their eyes.

Uncle nibbled again. The light went out. Nibble –
on. Nibble – off.

"Marvellous!" he said. "A sun-stick, by all that's
dazzling! This will give those Ruddertails
something to think about!" He slipped it into his
backpack and looked at the kits who were
determined, but understandably nervous. "What
we are about to face may easily be the greatest
shake-up of our lives. So listen, while I go over the
battle plan."

Chapter 20

As expected, the full company of the Ruddertails arrived soon after the sun lit up Shepherd Tree Clump. They were led by King Leaper. He was, as Uncle had warned, even bigger and more cruel-looking than Twisted Claw. A vivid stripe seemed to split his domed skull in two and his jaw opened and closed ceaselessly, displaying long, deadly fangs. His eye-patches ran into deep, black, narrow caves almost from his twitching nostril to his tattered ears. His movements were always quick and threatening and his deep, staring eyes challenged everything in their view. Leaper moved among his restless troops as they presented themselves straight after Warm-up under the spreading branches of their gathering place. Briskly he scent-marked all his followers, never pausing until all thirty-seven of them carried his powerful stink. To judge by the grunt of pride that each Ruddertail gave as they were squirted, he might have been dressing them in bite-proof armour.

"Ruddertails! Show your rudders!" cried Leaper and at once a forest of red-tipped tails rose like bloody spears. They bustled about like a moving stockade, screaming and dancing. Then they rushed forward until they were not much more than a leopard's leap from the main entrance to Far Burrow.

What stopped them was a small, feeble-looking little female. She stepped out from the shadowy mouth of the burrow and boldly blocked the entrance with her skinny body. The Ruddertail army hooted with laughter, screamed insults. They waved their tails, made little pretend charges and hopped up and down menacingly. They were a bit worried by the coloured material she had wrapped round her – but there were so many of them, they felt sure they could soon shoo her away like a spider.

To their surprise, the strange little thing took no notice at all. Instead, she stood alone in the bright sun, calmly lifted her tummy – HUP! – and warmed herself. The noise and the war dancing grew louder and wilder. She simply smiled and waved at them as if they were friends and then began to hop and skip about. She dug a little play-mound (which she jumped on and off) then she did a roly-poly and sang quietly to herself.

The Ruddertails grew frantic and stampeded

about. But since the little kit did not seem in the least bothered, they gradually ran out of puff. Finally they slowed down to a gentle jog. "Hold your positions, Ruddertails!" came the commanding voice of King Leaper. "Save your energy! Can't you see that this little kit is too mad or stupid to be frightened? Leave her be and stand by until we see exactly what kind of army the enemy can bring out to challenge us! Wait for my signal to charge."

Mimi was pleased with the way things had gone so far. Next, she took off her dress and tied it to a stick. As the breeze picked up, it began to flicker and crack in the breeze like the flags that the Blah-blahs flew over their pointy mounds. As soon as Mimi planted the stick in the sand, it came to life once more. It shimmered a brightly-coloured warning. "Do not touch me!" it seemed to say. "I am an unknown enemy. Bite me and my poison will make you scream and die."

"Oo-er! W-w-what's she doing?" a nervous young Ruddertail asked his neighbour.

"I dunno!" came the anxious reply. "But I don't like the way that flat creature looks at you! And listen to him snapping. That's dangerous, that is!"

Mimi then dug just below the mound she had made and uncovered two canisters…

"Now what?" came the worried voice.

"What are those two shiny things she's dug up?"

Mimi batted them about, rolled them gingerly. Then she grabbed one between her teeth and shook it like a rat. She dropped it, backed away, crept up to it, put her ear against it and let out a piercing scream, "Spit, cobra, spit!"

It was a dreadful noise and the Ruddertails all shuffled back a little when they heard it. They turned to their king, not knowing what to do next. Then they saw Mimi hook a claw under the ring at one end of the canister. It gave a frightful

Hisss**SS**! and shot brown venom

towards them. As one body, the attackers shrank

back with howls of fear. It took all Leaper's

courage to stay where he was. But he knew that if

he turned tail now, with the whole tribe expecting

him to set an example, his days as king would

soon be over. "We must push forward!" he cried.

"She may strike some of us with her poison, but the rest of us will win through! We need to get into the burrow quickly and chase out any Sharpeyes who are sheltering underground."

"Come on, then!" shouted one of his braver followers. "Forward, the Ruddertails!"

But before a charge could begin, another young Sharpeye warrior (Skeema – who else?) rushed out of the burrow, with a growl that was more like a leopard cub's than a meerkat's. Was he about to do battle with the Ruddertails? No! He was preparing for a fight with something deadly-looking! A nasty, lime-green Snap-snap, it was. It went for his front leg! What a struggle! Suddenly, the young meerkat flipped the Snap-snap high in the air and sank his teeth into its neck as it came down. It let out an ear-splitting SQUEAK!

"He's killed it!" cried one of the Ruddertails. He

was so impressed, he blurted out, "Well played, son!" and got soundly nipped by his mates.

The young Sharpeye sniffed the Snap-snap and lifted it up in his paws to mark his victory. Then – horror of horrors – the Snap-snap suddenly came to life again! It wriggled, it jumped high in the air! As it came down, the youngster tried to catch it, but it opened its terrible jaws and clamped them round his throat! The Ruddertails were shocked into silence as they watched the young Sharpeye fighting to save himself again. They half hoped he would hold on – but suddenly his legs gave way. He slipped. Slowly the Snap-snap tightened his jaws. Bit by bit he squeezed the breath out of the brave young struggler until he flopped lifeless on to the sand. He gave a final twitch and lay still. The Snap-snap's victory squeak was enough to make the blood run cold. But there was something really wicked about the way it suddenly flew up into the air, did a somersault, and dived straight back down the entrance to the burrow.

"Bull's-eye!" muttered Skeema to himself, pleased with his rather lucky throw. Then, it was time for a bit more acting. "ARRGHHH!" he gurgled, very theatrically. "My paws!" he yelled, howling with pain. He went wild. He jittered and juddered all over the sand. Then he sat up – and pulled off his desert boots!

There was shock among the Ruddertail ranks. "He's pulled his back feet off!" someone yelled. "I don't believe it! He's pulled 'em right off! And now look! He's chucking them up in the air!"

Not content with tearing off his own feet, he put his front paws up to his eyes – and pulled them out! He actually pulled out his shiny round eyes and flung *them* into the air. The sun caught them and made them sparkle for a second before they

183

plopped into the sand with two sickening thuds.

"Errr!" chorused the Ruddertail army. "Disgusting!"

They watched open-mouthed as the poor fellow wriggled like a skink to the entrance hole and slid himself down it. There followed another awful scream.

"That Snap-snap must have finished him off!" gasped an old-timer. "That poor little guy killed it, but then it came back to life! Then it poisoned him and sent him raving mad! And now it's finished him off!"

"I'm *definitely* not going down that burrow! Not with a spitting cobra *and* a Snap-snap down there!" replied his neighbour.

The king sensed the rising panic amongst his soldiers. "Keep your nerve, everyone!" he called. "Stand by to rush the burrow. We don't know for sure how many of them there are, but there can't be many. On the count of three, we'll charge

184

together. Are you all set? One… two…"

At the count of two, a *very* small meerkat with square shiny black eyes came charging out of the entrance to the burrow and ran straight at them. At first he seemed to be all on his own. Instead of the normal war cry, he shouted, "Wheeee!" as if he were having the time of his life.

"Tear him to pieces!" commanded Leaper. The Ruddertails flew towards him as one, teeth and claws at the ready. But the fact was, as they closed on Little Dream and looked into his eyes, he suddenly turned into a whole army with a forest of tails waving. Dozens of meerkats had suddenly appeared out of thin air, dancing and threatening!

The front rank of the Ruddertails staggered to a ragged halt, turned and ran into the ones behind. "What's the matter with you all? CHARGE!" screamed King Leaper.

That was the signal for yet more Sharpeye fighters to pop up from escape holes all around the burrow, dancing and yelling for all they were worth. Amazingly, the crazy little female was there again, another snake-weapon in her paw. The young male who had pulled out his eyes and torn off his feet had come back to life too! He was running along clutching the poisonous Snap-snap.

"Don't hang back, you fools!" screamed the King of the Ruddertails. "There are far more of us than them. CHARGE!"

The Ruddertail army was well-drilled and used to obeying orders. The warriors were nervous and upset, but still they gathered themselves into their fighting formation and prepared to rush the enemy. But once again, a wicked hissing snake sprang from the tube the little female was holding and spat great gobs of sticky brown poison high into the air. At the same time, a bolt of lightning

186

flashed from the chest of the littlest meerkat. How the Ruddertails howled and panicked! And when they uncovered their faces and looked up, they saw a sight not one of them would forget.

Chapter 21

A rider was charging down the side of the valley, trumpeting and raising a cloud of dust.

"An elephant!" someone yelled. "A pink elephant on the charge!"

"Look out!"

"Retreat! Head for the dunes! Take cover! Run for your lives!"

Uncle Fearless could only cling on to the galloping egg chamber. He was going in the right direction and he was doing a good job making trumpeting noises, but had no control over his mount. To tell the truth, it wasn't part of the plan for it to gather *quite* so much speed. By the time it hit the mound in front of the back entrance to Far Burrow, it was racing like a cheetah.

The egg chamber roared up the steep slope and took off. There was a moment's hush as it hung in the air… then slammed into the middle ground between the two armies – and burst open.

The egg that Uncle and the kits had wanted so much to return to its mamma was jerked free of its straps and rolled among the enemy warriors. Several of the Ruddertails were bowled over by it, like furry skittles. As the egg bounced along, the golden covering and the ribbon round it were ripped away.

Suddenly a monstrous creature was hatched! As it broke from its golden, shiny shell it was already flapping and calling a wild *Ooo-hoo-hoooo!*

It was an eagle owl!

Not one Ruddertail stayed around to see what happened next, but the kits saw it. Caked in dust and bruised all over, Uncle staggered to his feet. Blink as he might, he couldn't clear the muck from his one good eye. Dimly he saw the moving wings of… The Silent Enemy. He heard repeated the chilling *HOO-HOOO* of his attack-call. Until now this sound had always made Fearless tremble and turned his insides to jelly. Yet now he felt nothing but rage.

"So, you have come back for the kits!" he cried. "You think you can take them when their minds are busy with thoughts of the Ruddertails! But you'll have to get past me first, what-what!"

Furiously he leapt at his arch-enemy, exclaiming, "Do your worst with your nasty beak and talons! This time, we fight to the death!" And with that, he grabbed the eagle owl and shook the daylights out of him! Feathers and fluff and stuffing flew, but Fearless the Bold battled on, ripping and twisting.

"*We love you, Charlie!*" sang the eagle owl in two voices that sounded like Blah-blah calls.

"Aha! Not so silent now, are you?" yelled Uncle.

"*Happy birthday to our best little boy,*" said the

voices of the eagle owl. "*We hope you have a wonderful holiday and see lots of meerkats!*"

Uncle wasn't put off by this frightening, meaningless babble. He never gave up the struggle until he had the hard, dark heart of his arch-enemy in his jaws.

Even then, it seemed determined to have a last word:

> *"Happy birthday to you,"*

sang the heart.

> *"Happy birthday to you*
> *Happy birthday, dear Charlie*
> *Happy b—"*

One final crunch from Uncle's fiercely gritted teeth – and it was silenced forever.

Chapter 22

None of the fighters caught up in the battle noticed, but a party of Blah-blahs had been filming the whole thing. Apart from the cameraman and the soundman, there was a TV presenter, his wife and their little boy.

As the last of the screaming Ruddertails galloped back beyond the Salt Pans, never to return, the watchers stepped out of their hiding place and looked with amazement at the wreckage on the battlefield.

"I say!" gasped the woman. "You said we might

see a bit of action, but – my goodness! – that was extraordinary!" She turned to the little boy. "Wasn't it, Charlie, dear? Aren't you glad we came to see Daddy at work? And on your birthday, too!"

The little boy at her side put his thumb in his mouth and nodded. She picked him up and hugged him.

"Did you get all that, chaps?" the presenter asked the film crew. "I do hope so because that was the most amazing behaviour we've seen so far!"

"Don't worry, it's all on film," said the cameraman, whose name was Nick. "How was the sound, Jack?"

"It was all too far away to hear much," said the soundman. "But I'll play some of it back." He flipped a switch and it was just possible to hear a tinny voice singing *Happy birthday to you…*

"How very strange!" said the woman in a

shocked whisper. "Feedback, I suppose…"

Her husband wasn't paying attention though. He had stooped and picked something up. "Do you know, sweetheart," he said, "some of these things scattered around look just like Charlie's! This travel torch, for example." He explored a little further and picked up something else. "And look here! Here's a glass marble. Charlie had a little collection in a matchbox, remember? And here's a picture book and an opened packet of jelly beans! Well I never! This is exactly like the stuff we packed in Charlie's suitcase."

"Yes, but darling, the suitcase fell off the roof of the jeep somewhere *miles* from here. You remember… when we got caught in that sandstorm on our way to our way back to camp and got completely lost?"

"Daddy! Look over here!" wailed Charlie pointing down the other side of the sand dune he was standing on top of. "Somebody broke my elephant case!" And he burst into tears.

"Oh, don't cry on your birthday, Charlie! We'll get you another pull-along to keep your things in," soothed his mother.

The presenter was bending over something else he had discovered. "Well, now this is just *incredible*! Look what I've just found. It's the remains of the SPEKE-TO-ME eagle owl toy we bought Charlie as a birthday present! It's been ripped to shreds. What a pity! After all the trouble we took to record a heartbeat and a birthday message! Here's the speaker, look – and the batteries. I'm afraid one of the meerkats must have thought it was the real thing and attacked it!"

"That's not surprising when you remember that the eagle owl is one of the meerkat's most successful predators," his wife reminded him.

"What *is* surprising is that all Charlie's belongings have turned up here!"

Charlie looked blankly at the mess and his sobs turned to a snivel. Something had caught his attention. Flying from a stick planted on a little heap of sand was the ragged piece of soft coloured cloth. Once it had been Mimi's dress and now it was a battle flag.

Charlie's round, angry face lit up at last. His mouth stretched into a proper birthday smile. "MY NOO-NOO!" he beamed and snatched it into his arms.

In went his thumb. He scrunched his long-lost

noo-noo softly against his cheek, sat down and closed his eyes. *Nung nung nung.* Bliss!

His mummy and daddy came and sat down beside him. They looked at each other and smiled. "I think that's probably the best birthday present you've ever had, isn't it, Charlie?" she said. Their little boy nodded, his eyes still tight shut with happiness.

Meanwhile his dad had noticed that one of the meerkats was stretched out on the battlefield. It lay quite still. "What a shame!" he said to himself. "I do hope he's not too badly hurt." Quietly, he made his way towards it.

When the man was just a step away, Uncle Fearless began to stir. His whiskers twitched, he blinked and he rolled on to his side.

"Hush!" whispered the presenter, placing his finger to his lips to warn the others. "This poor old meerkat must have been knocked cold. I think he's just beginning to come round." He lifted his camera to his eye and looked through the viewfinder at the dazed creature. "I'd like to get some close-ups. Don't make any sudden moves now or you'll frighten him."

Charlie stayed where he was and his mother knelt down in the sand beside him.

"Well, I'm blessed!" exclaimed the presenter softly. "This is quite astonishing! All this time I thought we'd lost the dear old boy – and here he is!" He signalled to his wife to bring the boy over to look. "This is His Majesty!" he whispered. He was obviously very moved. "The star of *Meerkats on the Move*! He's definitely the dominant male we spent such a long time filming for our last series. He's still wearing the radio collar I put on him, can you see?"

Tenderly he slid his hand under the cheek of the dazed little creature. What he saw clearly upset him. "Oh dear, the poor old fellow's face has been horribly injured, look. Can you see? He's lost one of his eyes. It looks like an old injury. He really has been through the wars, poor fellow. I do hope he's not going to slip away just when we've found him again."

"Are you sure that's His Majesty?" whispered his wife.

"I'm certain. I recognise him from the pattern of patches on his back. Come over here, Nick. Bring the camera, nice and steady. Jack, bring the microphone closer." Gently he stroked Fearless's cheek with his finger. Come on, old soldier. See if you can get up on your feet. It's me. Don't you remember me?" He made a click-click sound with his tongue. That did it! The meerkat twitched. All his senses jerked into action. He whipped his head round and opened his good eye...

"Blah-blahs!" said Fearless to himself. He saw

201

how they bowed down to him and hid their faces behind their eye-protecting boxes. "And I'd know that call anywhere!" He gazed up at the presenter. "Well, well! If it isn't my old friend and helper, the Chief of the Click-clicks!"

"Thank goodness!" exclaimed the presenter, as softly as he could when he was so excited. "He's coming round and I think he knows me! He doesn't seem at all afraid."

Uncle pulled himself to his full height and gave himself a shake-up. He turned and caught the scent of the kits in their hiding places and called for them to follow. Boldly and steadily, Uncle began to climb the leg of the presenter. The eyes of the wife and the child grew wide with wonder. They both stood up to watch.

"*Di-deet!*" called Uncle, and Skeema and Mimi threw caution to the winds and came

dashing along to do as he instructed. While
Uncle clambered right up on top of the
Blah-blah's head, the kits chose a slightly lower
perch on his shoulders.

"It's all true!" said Mimi, excitedly. "You
really can get the Blah-blahs to obey you!"

"I always knew it was true about your Glory Days," said Skeema. "Anyone can see you're a proper king and not just a pretend, secret one. And isn't it a wonderful view from up here, Dreamie?" He looked down for his brother but for a moment he couldn't see him.

Suddenly there was a cry of delight from the little boy. "Mummy! Mummy! Look what the littlest meerkat's doing! He's climbing up on to my head!" Charlie wasn't at all afraid. "Hello, little meerkat!" he whispered and reached up to give his tummy a tickle.

His mother's face lit up with a broad smile and all the meerkats had to hold tight as their human look-out posts shook with laughter.

"I love Far Burrow," cried Little Dream with a delighted laugh, as everyone curled up together in a freshly dug chamber, safe and cool in the darktime. "Is it ours now?"

"Well we won it, didn't we?" chuckled Uncle. "By hook *and* by crook, what-what!"

"And you can be King of the Sharpeyes again as well as King of the Blah-blahs!" said Skeema.

"Um, yes – well – look here!" said Uncle. "I for one should be delighted to start again, with my own little tribe. In which case, I really think we need to give ourselves a new name. Has anyone got any suggestions?"

Little Dream did have a suggestion, and a very good one.

And as the shepherd trees began to throw cool shadows across the entrance to their beautiful new burrow, a delighted little crowd of Click-clicks was huddled happily together round a computer. They were enjoying the first screening of a scene that would soon be shown all around the world. In it, a famous presenter was telling the viewers, with pride and delight, that his wife and little boy were privileged to be the very first look-out posts of a brand new meerkat clan.

"This delightful, brave old creature," he whispered, "is a very long way from his old home. "He has clearly suffered a dreadful injury, and may well have lost his place as leader of the Sharpeyes. But I'm happy to report that he's alive and well. And it looks very much as if he intends to start, here on the edge of the Salt Pans, a new life, with a brand new tribe…"

And of course he was right.

And for their fans all over the globe, here is the latest family picture of…

The Really Mad Mob.

Join Uncle Fearless, Mimi, Skeema
and Little Dream on a new desert
adventure...

More

Meerkat Madness

coming soon...